GREAT ILLUSTRATED CLASSICS

BEAUTY & THE BEAST
& Other Stories

BARONET BOOKS, New York, New York

GREAT ILLUSTRATED CLASSICS

edited by
Rochelle Larkin

Contents

His Money was Not Too Much.

BEAUTY · AND · THE · BEAST

O nce upon a time there lived a merchant who was enor-
mously rich. He had sons and daughters, and his money
was not too much for everything they fancied and were
accustomed to.

One day a most unexpected misfortune befell. Their house
caught fire and burnt to the ground, with all the splendid furniture,
and precious goods it contained; but this was only the beginning of
their troubles. The father, who had prospered in all ways, suddenly
lost every ship he had, either by pirates, shipwreck, or fire. Then he
heard that his clerks in distant countries, whom he trusted entirely,
were unfaithful; and from great wealth he fell into direst poverty.

All that was left was a little house in a desolate place far from
the town in which he had lived, and there he was forced to retreat,
his children in despair at leading such a different life. The daughters at first hoped that their friends, who had been so numerous,
would insist on their staying in their houses now that they no
longer possessed one. But they soon found that they were alone,

and that their former friends attributed their misfortunes to their own extravagance.

So nothing was left but to take to their cottage, in the midst of a dark forest that seemed the most dismal place on earth. They were too poor to have servants; the girls had to work like peasants, and the sons worked in the fields to earn their living.

The girls regretted unceasingly their former life; only the youngest tried to be brave and cheerful. When misfortune overtook her father, she worked to make the best of things, to amuse her father and brothers and to get her sisters to join her. But they would do nothing, and declared that this miserable life was all she was fit for.

But she was prettier and cleverer than they were; she was so lovely that she was called Beauty.

After two years their father heard that one of his ships, believed to be lost, had come safely to port with a rich cargo. They thought that their poverty was at an end, and wanted to set out directly for town; but their father, more prudent, begged them to wait a little, and determined to go himself first.

Only Beauty doubted that they would be as rich as before, or at least rich enough to live where they would find amusement and fine companions again. The rest of them asked their father for jewels and dresses which would have cost a fortune; only Beauty did not ask for anything.

Her father, noticing her silence, said: "And what shall I bring for you, Beauty?"

The Cottage in the Forest

"All I want is for you to come home safely," she answered.

This reply vexed her sisters, who fancied she was blaming them for having asked for costly things. Her father, however, was pleased, and told her to choose something.

"Dear father," she said, "will you bring me a rose? I have not seen one since we came here, and I love them so much."

The merchant reached town only to find that his former companions, believing him dead, had divided the ship's goods, and after months of trouble he found himself as poor as when he started, with only just enough to pay for the journey.

To make matters worse, he left in terrible weather, so that when he was within a few miles of home he was exhausted with cold and fatigue. Night overtook him as deep snow and bitter frost made it impossible to go any further.

Not a house was to be seen; the only shelter was a hollow tree trunk, where he crouched all the long night. In spite of his weariness, the howling wolves kept him awake, and when day broke, falling snow had covered everything and he did not know where to turn.

At length he made out some sort of track, and though it was so rough and slippery that he fell down more than once, it led him to an avenue of orange trees which ended at a splendid castle.

It seemed very strange that no snow had fallen in the avenue of orange trees, flowers, and fruit. When he saw a flight of agate steps, he went up and passed through several splendid rooms.

"Will You Bring Me a Rose?"

The pleasant warm air revived him, but there seemed to be nobody in this vast and splendid palace. Silence reigned everywhere, and at last, tired of roaming through empty rooms and galleries, he stopped in a room where a fire was burning, and a couch drawn cozily close to it. Thinking that this must be for someone who was expected, he sat down to wait, and soon fell into a sweet sleep.

When extreme hunger wakened him, he was still alone; a little table, on which was a good dinner, was set close to him, and, as he had eaten nothing for twenty-four hours, he lost no time in beginning his meal, hoping for an opportunity to thank his considerate host.

But no one appeared even after another long sleep, though a fresh meal of cakes and fruit was on the little table. The silence terrified him, and he searched once more through the rooms; but not even a servant was to be seen; there was no sign of life.

He began to wonder what he should do, and amused himself pretending that the treasures he saw were his, and how he would divide them among his children. He went down into the garden, and though it was winter everywhere else, here the sun shone, birds sang, flowers bloomed, and the air was soft and sweet.

The merchant said to himself: "All this must be meant for me. I will go and bring my children to share these delights."

When he reached the castle, he had taken his horse to the stable and fed it. Now he thought to saddle it for his homeward

Silence Reigned Everywhere.

journey, and went down the path to the stable. This path had a hedge of roses and the merchant thought he had never seen such exquisite flowers.

They reminded him of his promise to Beauty, and he had just gathered one for her when he was startled by a strange noise behind him. Turning round, he saw a frightful Beast, which said in a terrible voice:

"Who told you that you might gather my roses? Was it not enough that I allowed you in my palace and was kind to you? This is the way you show your gratitude, by stealing my flowers! But your insolence shall not go unpunished."

The merchant dropped the fatal rose and, throwing himself on his knees, cried: "Pardon me, noble sir. I am truly grateful for your hospitality, which was so magnificent that I could not imagine you offended by my taking such a little thing as a rose."

But the Beast's anger was not lessened. "You are very ready with excuses and flattery," he cried; "but that will not save you from the death you deserve."

"Alas!" thought the merchant, "if my daughter Beauty only knew what danger her rose has brought me into!" In despair he began to tell the Beast his misfortunes, and of his journey, and Beauty's request.

"A king's ransom would not have procured all that my other daughters asked," he said; "but I thought that I might at least take Beauty her rose. I beg you to forgive me, for I meant no harm."

"Stealing My Flowers!"

The Beast considered for a moment, and then said, in a less furious tone: "I will forgive you on one condition — that you give me one of your daughters."

"Ah!" cried the merchant, "if I were cruel enough to buy my own life at the expense of one of my children's, what excuse could I invent to bring her here?"

"No excuse would be necessary," answered the Beast. "She must come willingly. On no other condition will I have her. See if one is courageous enough, and loves you enough, to come and save your life. You seem an honest man, so I trust you and give you a month to see if one of your daughters will stay here, to let you go free. If none is willing, you will belong to me. If you fail to keep your word I will come and fetch you!"

The merchant accepted, though he did not think any of his daughters would come. He promised to return at the time appointed, and asked permission to set off at once.

But the Beast answered that he could not go until the next day. "Then you will find a horse ready for you," he said. "Now go and eat and await my orders."

The poor merchant, more dead than alive, went to his room, where the most delicious supper was on the little table before the blazing fire. But he was terrified and just tasted a few of the dishes, for fear the Beast should be angry if he did not obey his orders. When he heard a great noise, he knew the Beast was coming. As he could do nothing to escape this visit, he wanted to seem as little

"Give Me One of Your Daughters!"

afraid as possible; so when the Beast asked roughly if he had supped well, the merchant answered that he had, thanks to his host's kindness.

The Beast warned him to remember the agreement, and to prepare his daughter for what to expect. "Do not get up tomorrow," he added, "until you see the sun and hear a golden bell. You will find the horse you are to ride ready in the courtyard. She will bring you back when you come with your daughter a month hence. Farewell. Take a rose to Beauty, and remember your promise!"

The merchant could not sleep for sadness; he lay down until the sun rose. Then he went to gather Beauty's rose. His horse carried him so swiftly that he lost sight of the palace and was still wrapped in gloomy thoughts when it stopped at his cottage.

His sons and daughters rushed to meet him, eager to know of his journey, which, seeing him on a splendid horse and in a rich mantle, they supposed to be favorable. But he hid the truth from them at first, only saying sadly to Beauty as he gave her the rose:

"Here is what you asked me to bring you; you little know what it has cost."

He told his adventures from beginning to end, and the daughters lamented their lost hopes, and the sons declared that their father should not return and began to make plans for killing the Beast if it should come to fetch him. But he reminded them that he had promised to go back.

His Horse Carried Him Swiftly.

Beauty said to them: "I have indeed caused this misfortune, but I did it innocently. Who could guess that to ask for a rose in the middle of summer would cause so much misery? But as I did, it is only just that I should suffer for it. I will therefore go back with my father to keep his promise."

At first her father and brothers declared that nothing could make them let her go; but Beauty was firm. She gave her little possessions to her sisters, and said goodbye to everything she loved, and when the fatal day came she encouraged and cheered her father as they mounted the horse which had brought him back.

It seemed to fly rather than gallop, but Beauty was not frightened; indeed, she would have enjoyed it if she had not feared the end.

Her father still tried to persuade her to go back, but in vain. While the night fell, to their great surprise, colored lights shone, and fireworks blazed out before them; the forest was illuminated, and even felt pleasantly warm, though it had been bitterly cold before.

They reached the orange trees, where statues were holding flaming torches, and when they got nearer the palace it was illuminated from the roof to the ground, and music sounded softly from the courtyard.

"The Beast must be very hungry," said Beauty, trying to laugh, "if he makes all this rejoicing over the arrival of his prey." But she could not help admiring all she saw.

"It is Only Just I Suffer for It."

The horse stopped at the terrace, and her father led her to the little room he had been in before, where they found a fire burning, and the table set with a delicious supper.

They had hardly finished when the Beast's footsteps were heard, and Beauty clung to her father in terror, which became all the greater when she saw how frightened he was. But when the Beast appeared, though she trembled at the sight of him, she made a great effort and saluted him respectfully.

This pleased the Beast. After looking at her he said, in a tone that might have struck terror into the boldest heart, though he did not seem to be angry: "Good evening, old man. Good evening, Beauty."

Beauty answered sweetly: "Good evening, Beast."

"Have you come willingly?" asked the Beast. "Will you be content to stay here when your father goes away?"

Beauty answered bravely that she was quite prepared to stay.

"I am pleased with you," said the Beast. "As you have come of your own accord, you may stay. As for you," he added, turning to the merchant, "sunrise tomorrow is your departure. When the bell rings you will find the same horse waiting to take you home; you must never expect to see my palace again."

Then turning to Beauty, he said: "Take your father into the next room, and choose everything your brothers and sisters would like to have. You will find travelling-trunks there; fill them full as you can. It is only just to send them something very

She Made a Great Effort.

precious as a remembrance of yourself."

Then he went away, after saying, "Good-bye, Beauty; good-bye, old man;" and though Beauty was filled with great dismay, she was afraid to disobey the Beast. They went into the next room, greatly surprised at all its riches. There were splendid dresses fit for a queen, with all their ornaments; when Beauty opened the cupboards she was dazzled by the jewels that lay in heaps on every shelf.

After choosing a vast quantity for her sisters, she opened the last chest, which was full of gold.

"I think, father," she said, "that, as the gold will be more useful, we had better take out the other things and fill the trunks with gold." So they did; but the more they put in, the more room there seemed to be, and they put back all the jewels and dresses and Beauty added as many more of the jewels as she could carry at once; and even then the trunks were not too full, but so heavy an elephant could not have carried them!

"The Beast was mocking us," cried the merchant, "he pretended to give us all these, knowing that I could not carry them!"

"Let us see," answered Beauty. "I cannot believe he meant to deceive us. All we can do is to leave them ready."

They did, and returned to the little room where they found breakfast ready. The merchant ate with good appetite, as the Beast's generosity made him believe that he might perhaps venture to come back soon and see Beauty.

Fit for a Queen

But she was very sad when the bell rang sharply for the second time and warned them that the time was come to part. Down in the courtyard, two horses were waiting, one with the two trunks, the other to ride. They were pawing the ground in their impatience to start, and the merchant bid Beauty a hasty farewell; soon as he was mounted he went off at such a pace that she lost sight of him in an instant.

Then Beauty began to cry, and wandered sadly back to her own room. She lay down and instantly fell asleep.

And she dreamed she was walking by a brook bordered with trees, lamenting her sad fate, when a young Prince, more handsome than anyone she had ever seen, and with a voice that went straight to her heart, came and said to her: "Ah, Beauty! You are not so unfortunate as you suppose. Here you will be rewarded for all you have suffered. Your every wish shall be gratified. Only try to find me, no matter my disguise, as I love you dearly, and in making me happy you will find your own happiness. Be as true-hearted as you are beautiful, and we shall have nothing left to wish for."

"What can I do, Prince, to make you happy?" said Beauty.

"Only be grateful," he answered, "and do not trust too much to your eyes. And, above all, do not desert me until you have saved me from my cruel misery."

After this she found herself with a stately and beautiful lady, who said:

"Dear Beauty, do not regret all you have left behind, for you

A Young Prince

are destined to a better fate. Only do not be deceived by appearances."

Beauty found her dreams so interesting that she awoke, and sat down in the corner of a sofa, to think about the charming Prince in her dream.

"He said I could make him happy," said Beauty to herself. "It seems this Beast keeps him prisoner. Can I set him free? I wonder why they both told me not to trust appearances? But it was only a dream, so why trouble myself about it? Better to go and find something to amuse myself."

So she began to explore the many rooms of the palace. The first was lined with mirrors, and Beauty had never seen such a room. A bracelet hanging from a chandelier caught her eye. Taking it down she was greatly surprised to find that it held a portrait of her unknown admirer, just as he had looked in her dream.

She slipped the bracelet on her arm, and went into a picture gallery, where she found a portrait of the same handsome Prince. As she studied it, it seemed to smile at her.

Tearing herself away from the portrait at last, she went into a room with every musical instrument and amused herself trying them, and singing until she was tired.

The next room was a library, and a whole lifetime would not be enough to read the names of all the books, there were so many. By now it was dusk, and candles in diamond and ruby candlesticks were lighting themselves in every room.

Exploring the Rooms of the Palace

Beauty found her supper served, but she did not see anyone or hear a sound, and, though her father had warned her that she would be alone, she found it rather dull.

But presently she heard the Beast coming, and wondered tremblingly if he meant to eat her up now. However, as he did not seem at all ferocious, and only said gruffly: "Good-evening, Beauty," she answered cheerfully and managed to conceal her terror. The Beast asked how she had been amusing herself, and she told him all she had seen.

He asked if she could be happy in his palace; Beauty said everything was so beautiful that she would be very hard to please if she could not be happy. And after about an hour's talk Beauty began to think that the Beast was not nearly so terrible as she had supposed at first.

He got up to leave her, and asked in his gruff voice: "Do you love me, Beauty? Will you marry me?"

"Oh, I what shall I say?" cried Beauty, afraid to make the Beast angry by refusing.

"Say 'yes' or 'no' without fear," he replied.

"Oh! Then no, Beast," said Beauty hastily.

"Since you will not, good-night, Beauty," he said.

And she answered: "Good-night, Beast," very glad that her refusal had not provoked him. After he was gone she was very soon asleep, dreaming of her unknown Prince. She thought he came and said to her: "Ah, Beauty! Why are you so unkind to me? I fear

"Do You Love Me?"

I am fated to be unhappy for many a long day still."

Then her dreams changed, but the charming Prince figured in them all; when morning came she ran to the portrait to see if it was really like him, and she found that it certainly was.

In the morning Beauty amused herself in the garden, for the sun shone, and all the fountains were playing; but she was astonished to find it familiar to her, and when she came to the brook where she had first met the Prince in her dream, that made her think more than ever that he must be a prisoner of the Beast.

When she was tired she went back to the palace, and found a new room full of materials for every kind of work — ribbons to make into bows, and silks to work into flowers. There was an aviary full of rare birds, which were so tame that they flew to Beauty and perched on her shoulders and her hand.

"Pretty little creatures," she said, "how I wish that your cage was nearer my room, that I might hear you sing!" She opened a door, and found to her delight that it led into her own room, though she had thought it was the other side of the palace.

The days passed swiftly in different amusements. Every evening after supper the Beast came to see her, and always before saying good night, asked in his terrible voice: "Beauty, will you marry me?"

It seemed to Beauty, now that she understood him better, that when she said, "No, Beast," he went away quite sad. But her happy dreams of the handsome young Prince soon made her

She Ran to the Portrait.

forget the poor Beast, and the thing that disturbed her was to be constantly told to distrust appearances, to let her heart guide her, not her eyes; and many other perplexing things, which, try as she would, she could not understand.

So everything went on for a long time, until, happy as she was, Beauty longed for her father and brothers and sisters; and one night, seeing her sad look, the Beast asked what was the matter.

Beauty had quite ceased to be afraid of him. Now she knew he was really gentle in spite of his ferocious looks and his dreadful voice. So she answered that she was longing to see her home once more. On hearing this the Beast was distressed, and cried, "Ah! Beauty, have you the heart to desert an unhappy Beast like this? What more do you want to make you happy? Is it because you hate me that you want to escape?"

"No, dear Beast," answered Beauty softly, "I do not hate you, but I long to see my father again. Only let me go for two months, and I will come back to you for the rest of my life."

The Beast, sighing while she spoke, replied: "I cannot refuse you anything, even if it cost me my life. Take the four boxes in the room next to your own, and fill them with everything you wish to take with you. But remember your promise and come back when the two months are over, for if you do not, you will find your faithful Beast dead.

"All you will need to bring you back is to say good-bye to your brothers and sisters the night before, and to turn this ring

Beauty Longed for Her Father.

round upon your finger and say firmly: 'I wish to go back to my palace and see my Beast again.' Good-night, Beauty. Fear nothing, sleep peacefully, and before long you shall see your father once more."

As soon as Beauty was alone she hastened to fill the boxes with all the rare and precious things she saw about her; then she went to bed, but could hardly sleep for joy. When she did begin to dream of her beloved Prince, she was grieved to see him stretched upon a grassy bank sad and weary, and hardly like himself.

"What is the matter?" she cried.

But he looked at her reproachfully, and said: "How can you ask me, cruel one? Are you not leaving me to my death perhaps?"

"Ah! Don't be sorrowful," cried Beauty; "I only go to assure my father that I am safe and happy. I promised the Beast I will come back, and he would die of grief if I did not keep my word!"

"What would that matter to you?" said the Prince. "Surely you would not care?"

"Indeed I should be ungrateful if I did not care for such a kind Beast," cried Beauty indignantly. "I would die to save him from pain. I assure you it is not his fault that he is so ugly."

Just then a strange sound woke her — someone was speaking not very far away; and opening her eyes she found herself in a room she had never seen before, which was not nearly so splendid as those in the Beast's palace. Where could she be?

She got up and saw that the boxes she had packed the night

She Filled the Boxes.

before were all there. While she wondered by what magic the Beast had transported her to this strange place, she heard her father's voice, and rushed out and greeted him joyfully.

Her brothers and sisters were astonished at her appearance, as they had never expected to see her again, and there was no end to their questions. But when they heard that she had only come for a short time, and had to go back to the Beast's palace forever, they lamented loudly.

Beauty asked her father the meaning of her strange dreams, and why the Prince constantly begged her not to trust appearances. After much consideration he answered: "You tell me the Beast, frightful as he is, loves you dearly, and deserves your love and gratitude for his gentle kindness; the Prince must mean you ought to do as he wishes you to, in spite of his ugliness."

To Beauty, this seemed very probable; still, when she thought of her dear handsome Prince, she did not feel at all inclined to marry the Beast. At any rate, for two months she need not decide, but could enjoy herself with her brothers and sisters.

But though they were rich now, and lived in town again, and had plenty of acquaintances, Beauty found nothing that amused her much; she often thought of the palace, where she was so happy, especially as here she never once dreamed of her dear Prince, and she felt quite sad without him.

Every day when she got up she meant to say good-bye at night, but when night came she put it off again, until at last she

Her Brothers and Sisters Were Astonished.

had a dismal dream which helped make up her mind. She thought she was wandering in the palace gardens, when she heard groans from some bushes hiding a cave, and running quickly to see what was the matter, she found the Beast stretched out, apparently dying.

He reproached her with causing his distress, and at the same moment the stately lady appeared, and said very gravely: "You are only just in time to save his life. See what happens when people do not keep their promises! If you had delayed one day more, you would have found him dead."

Beauty was so terrified by this that the next morning she announced her intention of going back at once, and said good-bye to her father, her brothers, and sisters. As soon as she was in bed she turned her ring round upon her finger, and said firmly: "I wish to go back to my palace and see my Beast again," as she had been told to do.

She fell asleep and woke to hear the clock saying, "Beauty, Beauty," twelve times in its musical voice, which told her that she was in the palace once more. Everything was just as before, but Beauty had never known such a long day, for she was so anxious to see the Beast that she felt as if supper-time would never come.

But when it did come and no Beast appeared, she was really frightened; she ran into the garden to search for him. Up and down the paths ran Beauty, calling him in vain, for not a trace of him could she find; quite tired, she stopped for a minute's rest, and saw that she was standing in the path she had seen in her dream.

"I Wish to Go Back to My Beast."

She rushed down the path, and there was the cave, and in it the Beast — asleep, Beauty thought. She ran up and stroked his head, but to her horror he did not move or open his eyes.

"Oh! He is dead; and it is all my fault!" Beauty cried bitterly. But then, looking at him again, she fancied he still breathed, and, hastily fetching water from the nearest fountain, she sprinkled it over his face, and he began to revive.

"Oh! Beast, how you frightened me!" she cried. "I never knew how much I loved you until just now, when I feared I was too late to save your life."

"Can you really love such an ugly creature as I am?" said the Beast faintly. "Ah Beauty, you came only just in time. I was dying because I thought you had forgotten your promise. But go and I shall see you by and by."

Beauty, who had expected him to be angry with her, was reassured by his gentle voice, and went back to the palace. The Beast came in as usual, and talked about the time she had spent with her father.

Beauty answered politely, telling him all that had happened to her.

And when at last it was time for him to go, he asked, as he had so often before: "Beauty, will you marry me?"

"Yes, dear Beast," she answered softly.

As she spoke a blaze of light sprang up before the windows of the palace, fireworks crackled, and across the avenue of orange

"It is All My Fault."

trees, in letters all made of fire-flies, was written: "Long live the Prince and his Bride."

Turning to ask the Beast what it could mean, Beauty found in his place her long-loved Prince! At the same moment the wheels of a chariot were heard upon the terrace, and two ladies entered the room. One of them Beauty recognised as the stately lady she had seen in her dreams; the other was also so grand and queenly that Beauty hardly knew which to greet first.

But the one she already knew said to her companion:

"Queen, this is Beauty, who had the courage to rescue your son from the terrible enchantment. They love one another, and want only your consent to their marriage to make them perfectly happy."

"With all my heart," cried the Queen. "How can I ever thank Beauty enough for having restored my dear son to his natural form?"

She tenderly embraced Beauty and the Prince, who greeted the fairy and was receiving her congratulations.

"Now," said the fairy to Beauty, "I suppose you would like all your brothers and sisters to dance at your wedding?"

She did, and the marriage was celebrated with the utmost splendor, and Beauty and the Prince lived happily ever after.

In His Place, Her Long–Loved Prince!

The Most Lovely Garden

RAPUNZEL

From the Brothers Grimm

Once upon a time there lived a man and his wife who had no children. These good people had a little window at the back of their house, which looked into the most lovely garden, full of all manner of beautiful flowers and vegetables; but the garden was surrounded by a high wall, and no one dared to enter it, for it belonged to a witch of great power, who was feared by the whole world.

One day the woman stood at the window overlooking the garden, and saw there a bed full of the finest turnips: the leaves looked so fresh and green that she longed to eat them. Her desire grew day by day, and just because she knew she couldn't possibly get any, she pined away and became quite pale and wretched. Then her husband grew alarmed and said:

"What ails you, dear wife?"

"Oh," she answered, "if I don't get some turnips to eat out of the garden behind the house, I know I shall die."

The man, who loved her dearly, thought to himself, "Come!

Rather than let your wife die you shall fetch her some turnips, no matter the cost." So at dusk he climbed over the wall into the witch's garden, and, hastily gathering a handful of turnip leaves, he returned with them to his wife.

She made them into a salad, which tasted so good that her longing for the forbidden food was greater than ever. If she were to know any peace of mind, there was nothing for it but that her husband should climb over the garden wall again, and fetch her some more. So at dusk over the wall he went, but when he reached the other side he drew back in terror, for there, standing before him, was the old witch.

"How dare you," she said, with a wrathful glance, "climb into my garden and steal my turnips like a common thief? You shall suffer for your foolhardiness."

"Oh!" he implored, "pardon my presumption; necessity alone drove me to the deed. My wife saw your turnips from her window, and conceived such a desire that she would certainly have died if her wish had not been gratified."

Then the witch's anger was a little appeased, and she said: "If it's as you say, you may take as many turnips away with you as you like, but on one condition — that you give me the child your wife will shortly bring into the world. All shall go well with it, and I will look after it like a mother."

The man in his terror agreed to everything she asked, and as soon as the child was born the witch appeared, and having given it

"How Dare You?"

the name of Rapunzel, she carried it off with her.

Rapunzel was the most beautiful child under the sun. When she was twelve years old the witch shut her up in a tower in the middle of a great wood, which had neither stairs nor doors, only high up at the very top a small window. When the old witch wanted to get in she stood underneath and called out:

> "Rapunzel, Rapunzel,
> Let down your hair,"

for Rapunzel had wonderful long hair, and it was as fine as spun gold. Whenever she heard the witch's voice she unloosed her braids, and let her hair fall down out of the window about twenty yards below, and the old witch climbed up by it.

After they had lived like this for a few years, it happened one day that a Prince was riding through the wood and passed by the tower. As he drew near it he heard someone singing so sweetly that he stood spell-bound and listened. It was Rapunzel in her loneliness trying to while away the time by letting her sweet voice ring out into the wood.

The Prince longed to see the owner of the voice, but he sought in vain for a door in the tower. He rode home, but he was so haunted by the song he had heard that he returned every day to the wood and listened.

One day, when he was standing thus behind a tree, he saw the old witch approach and heard her call out:

> "Rapunzel, Rapunzel,

"Rapunzel, Rapunzel, Let Down Your Hair."

Let down your hair."

Then Rapunzel let down her braids, and the witch climbed up by them.

"So that's the staircase, is it?" said the Prince. "Then I too will climb it and try my luck."

On the following day at dusk, he went to the foot of the tower and cried:

"Rapunzel, Rapunzel,
Let down your hair,"

and as soon as she had let it down the Prince climbed up.

At first Rapunzel was terribly frightened when a man came in, for she had never seen one before; but the Prince spoke to her so kindly, and told her at once that his heart had been so touched by her singing, that he felt he should know no peace of mind till he had seen her.

Very soon Rapunzel forgot her fear, and when he asked her to marry him she consented at once. "For," she thought, "he is young and handsome, and I will certainly be happier with him than with the old witch."

So she put her hand in his and said:

"Yes, I will gladly go with you, only how am I to get down out of the tower? Every time you come to see me you must bring a skein of silk with you, and I will make a ladder of them, and when it is finished I will climb down by it, and you will take me away on your horse."

"Then I Too Will Climb It."

They arranged that, till the ladder was ready, he was to come to her every evening, because the old woman was with her during the day.

The old witch, of course, knew nothing of what was going on, till one day Rapunzel, not thinking of what she was about, turned to the witch and said: "How is it, good mother, that you are so much harder to pull up than the young Prince? He is always with me in a moment."

"Oh! You wicked child," cried the witch. "What is this I hear? I thought I had hidden you safely from the whole world, and in spite of it you have managed to deceive me!"

In her wrath she seized Rapunzel's beautiful hair, wound it round and round her left hand, and then grasping a pair of scissors in her right, snip snap, off it came, and the beautiful braids lay on the ground. And, worse than this, she was so hard-hearted that she took Rapunzel to a lonely desert place, and there left her to live in loneliness and misery.

But on the evening of the day in which she had driven poor Rapunzel away, the witch fastened the braids on to a hook in the window, and when the Prince came and called out:

"Rapunzel, Rapunzel,
Let down your hair,"

she let them down, and the Prince climbed up as usual, but instead of his beloved Rapunzel he found the old witch, who fixed her evil, glittering eyes on him, and cried mockingly:

"What Is This I Hear?"

"Ah, ah! You thought to find your lady love, but the pretty bird has flown and its song is dumb; the cat caught it, and will scratch out your eyes, too. Rapunzel is lost to you forever — you will never see her again."

The Prince was beside himself with grief, and in his despair he jumped right down from the tower, and, though he escaped with his life, the thorns among which he fell pierced his eyes. Then he wandered through the wood, blind and miserable, eating nothing but roots and berries, and weeping and lamenting the loss of his lovely bride. So he wandered about for some years, as wretched and unhappy as he could be, when at last he came to the desert place where Rapunzel was living.

Of a sudden he heard a voice which seemed strangely familiar to him. He walked eagerly in the direction of the sound, and when he was quite close, Rapunzel recognized him and fell on his neck and wept.

Two of her tears touched his eyes, and in a moment they became quite clear again, and he saw as well as he had ever done. Then he led her to his kingdom, where they were received and welcomed with great joy, and they lived happily ever after.

Then He Led Her to His Kingdom.

"Put It in a Flowerpot."

THUMBELINA

By Hans Christian Andersen

There was once a woman who wanted to have quite a tiny little child, but she did not know where to get one from. So one day she went to an old witch and said to her: "I should so much like to have a tiny little child; can you tell me where I can get one?"

"Oh, we have just got one ready!" said the witch. "Here is a barley-corn for you, but it's not the kind the farmer sows in his field, or feeds the hens with, I can tell you. Put it in a flowerpot, and then you will see something happen."

"Oh, thank you!" said the woman, and gave the witch a shilling, for that was what it cost. Then she went home and planted the barley-corn; immediately there grew out of it a large and beautiful flower, which looked like a tulip, but the petals were as tightly closed as if it were still only a bud.

"What a beautiful flower!" exclaimed the woman, and she kissed the red and yellow petals; and as she kissed them the flower burst open. It was a real tulip, such as one can see any day; but in the middle of the blossom, on the green velvety petals, sat a little girl, quite tiny, trim, and pretty. She was scarcely half a thumb in height, so they called her Thumbelina.

An elegant polished walnut-shell served Thumbelina as a cradle, the blue petals of a violet were her mattress, and a rose-leaf her coverlet.

There she lay at night, but in the day-time she used to play about on the table; here the woman had put a bowl, surrounded by a ring of flowers, with their stalks in water, in the middle of which floated a great tulip petal, and on this Thumbelina sat, and sailed from one side of the bowl to the other, rowing herself with two white horse-hairs for oars. It was such a pretty sight! She could sing, too, with a voice more soft and sweet than had ever been heard before.

One night, when she was lying in her pretty little bed, an old toad crept in through a broken pane in the window. She was very ugly, clumsy, and clammy; she hopped on to the table where Thumbelina lay asleep under the red rose leaf.

"This would make a beautiful wife for my son," said the toad, taking up the walnut-shell with Thumbelina inside, and hopping with it through the window into the garden.

There flowed a great wide stream, with slippery and marshy banks; here the toad lived with her son. Ugh! How clammy he was, just like his mother! "Croak, croak, croak!" was all he could say when he saw the pretty little girl in the walnut-shell.

"A Beautiful Wife for My Son."

"Don't talk so loud, or you'll wake her," said the old toad. "She might escape us even now; she is as light as a feather. We will put her at once on a broad water-lily leaf in the stream. That will be quite an island for her, she is so small and light. She can't run away from us there, whilst we are preparing the guest-chamber under the marsh where she shall live."

Outside in the brook grew many water-lilies, with broad green leaves, which looked as if they were swimming about on the water. The leaf farthest away was the largest, and to this the old toad swam with Thumbelina in her walnut-shell.

The tiny Thumbelina woke up very early in the morning, and when she saw where she was she began to cry bitterly; for on every side of the great green leaf was water, and she could not get to the land.

The old toad was down under the marsh, decorating her room with rushes and yellow marigold leaves, to make it very grand for her new daughter-in-law; then she swam out with her ugly son to the leaf where Thumbelina lay. She wanted to fetch the pretty cradle to put it into the room before Thumbelina herself came there. The old toad bowed low in the water before her, and said: "Here is my son; you shall marry him, and live in great magnificence down under the marsh."

"Croak, croak, croak!" was all that the son could say. Then they took the neat little cradle and swam away with it; but Thumbelina sat alone on the great green leaf and wept, for she did not

She Began to Cry Bitterly.

want to live with the clammy toad, or marry her ugly son.

The little fishes swimming about under the water had seen the toad quite plainly, and heard what she had said; so they put up their heads to see the little girl. When they saw her, they thought her so pretty that they were very sorry she should go down with the ugly toad to live. "That must not happen," they said amongst themselves.

They assembled in the water round the green stalk which supported the leaf on which she was sitting, and nibbled the stem in two. Away floated the leaf down the stream, bearing Thumbelina far beyond the reach of the toad.

On she sailed past several towns, and the little birds sitting in the bushes saw her, and sang, "What a pretty little girl!" The leaf floated farther and farther away; thus Thumbelina left her native land.

A beautiful little white butterfly fluttered above her, and at last settled on the leaf. Thumbelina pleased him, and she, too, was delighted, for now the toads could not reach her, and it was so beautiful where she was travelling; the sun shone on the water and made it sparkle like the brightest silver. She took off her sash, and tied one end round the butterfly; the other end she fastened to the leaf, so that now it glided along with her faster than ever.

A great finch came flying past; he caught sight of Thumbelina, and in a moment he had flown off with her to a tree. The green leaf floated away down the stream, and the butterfly with it, for he was fastened to the leaf and could not get loose from it. Oh,

Away Floated the Leaf.

dear! How terrified poor little Thumbelina was when the finch flew off with her to the tree!

But she was especially distressed on the beautiful white butterfly's account, as she had tied him fast, so that if he could not get away he must starve to death. But the finch did not trouble himself about that; he sat down with her on a large green leaf, gave her the honey out of the flowers to eat, and told her that she was very pretty, although she wasn't in the least like a finch.

Later on, all the other finches who lived in the same tree came to pay calls; they examined Thumbelina closely, and remarked, "Why, she has two long legs! How very miserable!"

"She has no beak!" cried another.

"How ugly she is!" said all the lady finches — and yet Thumbelina was really very pretty.

The finch who had stolen her knew this very well; but when he heard all the ladies saying she was ugly, he began to think so too, and would not keep her; Thumbelina could go wherever she liked. So he flew down from the tree with her and put her on a daisy. There she sat and wept, because she was so ugly that the finch would have nothing to do with her; and yet she was the most beautiful creature imaginable, so soft and delicate, like the loveliest rose leaf.

The whole summer poor little Thumbelina lived alone in the great wood. She braided a bed for herself of blades of grass, and hung it up under a clover leaf, so that she was protected from the rain; she gathered honey from the flowers for food, and drank the

The Finch Flew Off With Her.

dew on the leaves every morning. Thus the summer and autumn passed, but then came winter — the long, cold winter.

All the birds who had sung so sweetly about her had flown away; the trees shed their leaves; the flowers died; the great clover leaf under which she had lived curled up, and nothing remained of it but the withered stalk. She was terribly cold, for her clothes were ragged, and she herself was so small and thin. Poor little Thumbelina! She would surely be frozen to death.

It began to snow, and every snow-flake that fell on her was to her as a whole shovelful thrown on one of us, for we are so big, and she was only an inch high. She wrapped herself round in a dead leaf, but it was torn in the middle and gave her no warmth; she was trembling with cold.

Just outside the wood where she was now living lay a great corn field. But the corn had been gone a long time; only the dry, bare stubble was left standing in the frozen ground. This made a forest for her to wander about in. All at once she came across the door of a field-mouse, who had a little hole under a corn stalk.

There the mouse lived warm and snug, with a store room full of corn, and a splendid kitchen and dining room. Poor little Thumbelina went up to the door and begged for a little piece of barley, for she had not had anything to eat for the last two days.

"Poor little creature!" said the field-mouse, for she was a kindhearted old thing at bottom. "Come into my warm room and have some dinner with me."

Then Came the Long, Cold Winter.

As Thumbelina pleased her, she said: "As far as I am concerned you may spend the winter with me; but you must keep my room clean and tidy, and tell me stories, for I like that very much."

And Thumbelina did all that the kind old field-mouse asked, and did it remarkably well, too.

"Now I am expecting a visitor," said the field-mouse one day; "my neighbor comes to call on me once a week. He is in better circumstances than I am, has great, big rooms, and wears a fine white velvet coat. If you could only marry him, you would be well provided for. But he is blind. You must tell him all the prettiest stories you know."

But Thumbelina did not trouble her head about him, for he was only a mole. He came and paid them a visit in his white velvet coat.

"He is so rich and so accomplished," the field-mouse told her. "His house is twenty times larger than mine; he possesses great knowledge, but he cannot bear the sun and the beautiful flowers and speaks slightingly of them, for he has never seen them."

Thumbelina had to sing to him, so she sang "Ladybird, ladybird, fly away home!" and other songs so prettily that the mole fell in love with her; but he did not say anything, as he was a very cautious man.

A short time before he had dug a long passage through the ground from his own house to that of his neighbor; in this he gave

"You May Spend the Winter with Me."

the field-mouse and Thumbelina permission to walk as often as they liked. But he begged them not to be afraid of the dead bird that lay in the passage: it was a real bird with beak and feathers, and must have died a little time ago, and now laid buried just where he had made his tunnel.

The mole took a piece of rotten wood in his mouth, for that glows like fire in the dark, and went in front, lighting them through the long dark passage. When they came to the place where the dead bird lay, the mole put his broad nose against the ceiling and pushed a hole through, so that the daylight could shine down.

In the middle of the path lay the swallow, his pretty wings pressed close to his sides, his claws and head drawn under his feathers; the poor bird had evidently died of cold. Thumbelina was very sorry, for she was very fond of all little birds; they had sung and twittered so beautifully to her all through the summer.

But the mole kicked him with his bandy legs and said: "Now he can't sing any more! It must be very miserable to be a little bird! I'm thankful that none of my little children are; birds always starve in winter."

"Yes, you speak like a sensible man," said the field-mouse, "what has a bird, in spite of all his singing, in the winter time? He must starve and freeze, and that must not be very pleasant for him, I must say!"

Thumbelina did not say anything; but when the other two

Where the Dead Bird Lay

had passed on she bent down to the bird, brushed aside the feathers from his head, and kissed his closed eyes gently. "Perhaps it was he that sang to me so prettily in the summer," she thought. "How much pleasure he did give me, dear little bird!"

The mole closed up the hole which let in the light, and he then escorted the ladies home. But Thumbelina could not sleep that night; so she got out of bed, and braided a great big blanket of straw, and carried it off, and spread it over the dead bird, and piled upon it thistle-down as soft as cotton-wool, which she had found in the field-mouse's room, so that the poor little thing should lie warmly buried.

"Farewell, pretty little bird!" she said. "Farewell, and thank you for your beautiful songs in the summer, when the trees were green, and the sun shone down warmly on us!" Then she laid her head against the bird's heart. But the bird was not dead: he had been frozen, but now that she had warmed him, he was coming to life again.

In autumn the swallows fly away to foreign lands; but there are some who are late in starting, and then they get so cold that they drop down as if dead, and the snow comes and covers them over.

Thumbelina trembled, she was so frightened; for the bird was very large in comparison with herself — only an inch high. But she took courage, piled the down more closely over the poor swallow, fetched her own coverlet and laid it over his head.

The next night she crept out again to him. There he was

"Farewell, Pretty Little Bird!"

alive, but very weak; he could only open his eyes for a moment and look at Thumbelina, who was standing in front of him with a piece of rotten wood in her hand, for she had no other lantern.

"Thank you, pretty little child!" said the swallow to her. "I am so beautifully warm! Soon I shall regain my strength, and then I shall be able to fly out again into the warm sunshine."

"Oh!" she said, "It is very cold outside; it is snowing and freezing! Stay in your warm bed; I will take care of you!"

Then she brought him water in a petal, which he drank, after which he related to her how he had torn one of his wings on a bramble, so that he could not fly as fast as the other swallows, who had flown far away to warmer lands. So at last he had dropped down exhausted, and then he could remember no more.

The whole winter he remained in the tunnel, and Thumbelina looked after him and nursed him tenderly. Neither the mole nor the field-mouse learnt anything of this, for they could not bear the poor swallow.

When the spring came, and the sun warmed the earth again, the swallow said farewell to Thumbelina, who opened the hole in the roof for him which the mole had made. The sun shone brightly down upon her, and the swallow asked her if she would go with him; she could sit upon his back. Thumbelina wanted very much to fly far away into the green wood, but she knew that the old field-mouse would be sad if she ran away. "No, I mustn't come!" she said.

"Thank You, Pretty Little Child!"

"Farewell, dear good little girl!" said the swallow, and flew off into the sunshine. Thumbelina gazed after him with the tears standing in her eyes, for she was very fond of the swallow.

"Tweet, tweet!" sang the bird, and flew into the green wood. Thumbelina was very unhappy. She was not allowed to go out into the warm sunshine. The corn which had been sowed in the field over the field-mouse's home grew up high into the air, and made a thick forest for the poor little girl, who was only an inch high.

"Now you are to be a bride, Thumbelina!" said the field-mouse, "for our neighbor has proposed to you. What a piece of fortune for a poor child like you! Now you must set to work at your linen for your dowry, for nothing must be lacking if you are to become the wife of our neighbor, the mole!"

Thumbelina had to spin all day long, and every evening the mole visited her, and told her that when the summer was over the sun would not shine so hot; now it was burning the earth as hard as a stone. Yes, when the summer had passed, they would keep the wedding.

But she was not at all pleased about it, for she did not like the mole. Every morning when the sun was rising, and every evening when it was setting, she would steal out of the house door, and when the breeze parted the ears of corn so that she could see the blue sky through them, she thought how bright and beautiful it must be outside, and longed to see her dear swallow again. But he never came; no doubt he had flown away far into the great wood.

"Now You Are to be a Bride!"

By the autumn Thumbelina had finished the dowry.

"In four weeks you will be married!" said the field-mouse. "Don't be obstinate, or I shall bite you with my sharp white teeth! You will get a fine husband! The King himself has not such a velvet coat. His store-room and cellar are full, and you should be thankful for that."

Well, the wedding-day arrived. The mole had come to fetch Thumbelina to live with him deep down under the ground, never to come out into the warm sun again, for that was what he didn't like. The poor little girl was very sad, for now she must say good-bye to the beautiful sun.

"Farewell, bright sun!" she cried, stretching out her arms towards it, and taking another step outside the house; for now the corn had been reaped, and only the dry stubble was left standing. "Farewell, farewell!" she said, and put her arms round a little red flower that grew there. "Give my love to the dear swallow when you see him!"

"Tweet, tweet!" sounded in her ear all at once.

She looked up. There was the swallow flying past! As soon as he saw Thumbelina, he was very glad. She told him how unwilling she was to marry the ugly mole, as then she had to live underground where the sun never shone, and she could not help bursting into tears.

"The cold winter is coming now," said the swallow. "I must fly away to warmer lands: will you come with me? You can sit on my

Goodbye to the Beautiful Sun

back, and we will fly far away from the ugly mole and his dark house, over the mountains, to the warm countries where the sun shines more brightly than here, where it is always summer, and there are always beautiful flowers. Do come with me, dear little Thumbelina, who saved my life when I lay frozen in the dark tunnel!"

"Yes, I will go with you," said Thumbelina, and got on the swallow's back, with her feet on one of his outstretched wings. Up he flew into the air, over woods and seas, over the great mountains where the snow is always lying. And if she was cold she crept under his warm feathers, only keeping her little head out to admire all the beautiful things in the world beneath.

At last they came to warm lands; there the sun was brighter, the sky seemed twice as high, and in the hedges hung the finest green and purple grapes; in the woods grew oranges and lemons: the air was scented with myrtle and mint, and on the roads were pretty little children running about and playing with great gorgeous butterflies.

But the swallow flew on farther, and it became more and more beautiful. Under the most splendid green trees beside a blue lake stood a glittering white-marble castle. Vines hung about the high pillars; there were many swallows' nests, and in one of these lived the swallow who was carrying Thumbelina.

"Here is my house!" said he. "But it won't do for you to live with me; I am not tidy enough to please you. Find a home for yourself in one of the lovely flowers that grow down there; now I

"Yes, I Will Go With You."

will set you down, and you can do whatever you like."

"That will be splendid!" said she, clapping her little hands.

There lay a great white marble column which had fallen to the ground and broken into three pieces, but between these grew the most beautiful white flowers. The swallow flew down with Thumbelina, and set her upon one of the broad leaves.

But there, to her astonishment, she found a tiny little man sitting in the middle of the flower, as white and transparent as if he were made of glass; he had the prettiest golden crown on his head, and the most beautiful wings on his shoulders; he himself was no bigger than Thumbelina.

He was the spirit of the flower. In each blossom there dwelt a tiny man or woman; but this one was the King over the others.

"How handsome he is!" whispered Thumbelina to the swallow.

The little King was very much frightened at the swallow, for in comparison with one so tiny as himself he seemed a giant. But when he saw Thumbelina, he was delighted, for she was the most beautiful girl he had ever seen. So he took his golden crown from off his head and put it on hers, asking her name, and if she would be his wife, and then she would be Queen of all the flowers.

Yes! He was a different kind of husband than the son of the toad or the mole with the white velvet coat. So she said, "Yes!" to the noble King.

And out of each flower came a lady and gentleman, each so

A Little Man in the Middle of the Flower

tiny and pretty that it was a pleasure to see them. Each brought Thumbelina a present, but the best of all was a beautiful pair of wings which were fastened on to her back, and now she too could fly from flower to flower.

They all wished her joy, and the swallow sat above in his nest and sang the wedding march, and that he did as well as he could; but he was sad, because he was very fond of Thumbelina and did not want to be separated from her.

"You shall not be called Thumbelina!" said the King to her. "That is an ugly name, and you are much too pretty for that. We will call you May Blossom."

"Farewell, farewell!" said the little swallow with a heavy heart, and flew away to farther lands, far, far away, back north. There he had a little nest above a window, where his wife lived, who can tell fairy stories. "Tweet, tweet!" he sang to her. And that is the way we learnt the whole story.

A Beautiful Pair of Wings

The Star Gazer

THE · TWELVE · DANCING · PRINCESSES

O nce upon a time there lived a little cow-boy, without either father or mother. His real name was Michael, but he was always called the Star Gazer, because when he drove his cows over the commons to seek for pasture, he went along with his head in the air, gaping at nothing.

As he had white skin, blue eyes, and hair that curled all over his head, the village girls used to cry after him, "Well, Star Gazer, what are you doing?" And Michael would answer, "Oh, nothing," and go on his way without even turning to look at them.

The fact was he thought them very ugly, with their sun-burnt necks, their great red hands, their coarse petticoats and their wooden shoes. He had heard that somewhere in the world there were girls whose necks were white and whose hands were small, who were always dressed in the finest silks and laces, and were called Princesses, and while his companions round the fire saw nothing in the flames but common everyday fancies, he dreamed that he had the happiness to marry a Princess.

One morning about the middle of August, just at mid-day when the sun was hottest, Michael ate his piece of dry bread, and went to sleep under an oak. And while he slept he dreamt that there appeared before him a beautiful lady, dressed in a robe of gold, who said to him: "Go to the castle of Belloy, and there you shall marry a Princess."

That evening the little cow-boy, who had been thinking a great deal about the advice of the lady in the golden dress, told his dream to the farm people. But, as was natural, they only laughed at the Star Gazer.

The next day at the same hour he went to sleep again under the same tree. The lady appeared to him a second time, and said: "Go to the castle of Belloy, and you shall marry a Princess."

In the evening, Michael told his friends that he had dreamed the same dream again, but they only laughed at him more than before. "Never mind," he thought to himself; "if the lady appears to me a third time, I will do as she tells me."

The following day, to the great astonishment of all the village, about two o'clock in the afternoon a voice was heard singing:

"Raleô, raleô,
  How the cattle go!"

It was the little cow-boy driving his herd back to the barn.

The farmer began to scold him furiously, but he answered

"Go to the Castle of Belloy..."

quietly, "I am going away," made his clothes into a bundle, said good-bye to all his friends, and boldly set out to seek his fortune.

There was great excitement through all the village, and on the top of the hill the people stood holding their sides laughing, as they watched the Star Gazer trudging bravely along the valley with his bundle at the end of his stick.

It was well known for full twenty miles round that there lived in the castle of Belloy twelve Princesses of wonderful beauty, and as proud as they were beautiful, and who were besides so very sensitive and of such truly royal blood, that they would have felt at once the presence of a pea in their beds, even if twelve mattresses had been laid over it.

It was whispered about that they led exactly the lives that Princesses ought to lead, sleeping far into the morning, and never getting up till mid-day. They had twelve beds all in the same room, but what was very extraordinary was the fact that though they were locked in by triple bolts, every morning their satin shoes were found worn into holes.

When they were asked what they had been doing all night, they always answered that they had been asleep; and, indeed, no noise was ever heard in the room, yet the shoes could not wear themselves out alone!

At last the Duke of Belloy ordered the trumpet to be sounded. A proclamation was made that whoever could discover how his daughters wore out their shoes should choose one of

The Star Gazer Trudging Bravely Along

them for his wife.

On hearing the proclamation a number of Princes arrived at the castle to try their luck. They watched all night behind the open door of the Princesses, but when the morning came they had all disappeared, and no one could tell what had become of them.

When he reached the castle, Michael went straight to the gardener and offered his services. Now it happened that the garden boy had just been sent away, and though the Star Gazer did not look very sturdy, the gardener agreed to take him, as he thought that his pretty face and golden curls would please the Princesses.

The first thing he was told was that when the Princesses got up he was to present each one with a bouquet, and Michael thought that if he had nothing more unpleasant to do than that he should get on very well.

Accordingly he placed himself behind the door of the Princesses' room, with the twelve bouquets in a basket. He gave one to each of the sisters, and they took them without even deigning to look at the lad, except Lina the youngest, who fixed her large black eyes as soft as velvet on him, and exclaimed, "Oh, how pretty he is — our new flower boy!" The rest all burst out laughing, and the eldest pointed out that a Princess ought never to lower herself by looking at a garden boy.

Now Michael knew quite well what had happened to all the Princes, but notwithstanding, the beautiful eyes of the Princess Lina inspired him with a violent longing to try his fate. Unhappily

A Number of Princes Arrived at the Castle.

he did not dare to come forward, being afraid that he should only be jeered at, or even turned away from the castle on account of his impudence.

Nevertheless, the Star Gazer had another dream. The lady in the golden dress appeared to him once more, holding in one hand two young laurel trees, a cherry laurel and a rose laurel, and in the other hand a little golden rake, a little golden bucket, and a silken towel. She thus addressed him:

"Plant these two laurels in two large pots, rake them over with the rake, water them with the bucket, and wipe them with the towel. When they have grown as tall as a girl of fifteen, say to each of them, 'My beautiful laurel, with the golden rake I have raked you, with the golden bucket I have watered you, with the silken towel I have wiped you.' Then after that ask anything you choose, and the laurels will give it to you."

Michael thanked the lady in the golden dress, and when he woke he found the two laurel bushes beside him. So he carefully obeyed the orders he had been given.

The trees grew very fast, and when they were as tall as a girl of fifteen he said to the cherry laurel, "My lovely cherry laurel, with the golden rake I have raked thee, with the golden bucket I have watered thee, with the silken towel I have wiped thee. Teach me how to become invisible." Then there instantly appeared on the laurel a pretty white flower, which Michael gathered and stuck into his button-hole.

"Plant These Two Laurels."

That evening, when the Princesses went upstairs to bed, he followed them barefoot, so that he might make no noise, and hid himself under one of the twelve beds, so as not to take up much room.

The Princesses began at once to open their wardrobes and boxes. They took out of them the most magnificent dresses, which they put on before their mirrors, and when they had finished, turned themselves all round to admire their appearances.

Michael could see nothing from his hiding-place, but he could hear everything, and he listened to the Princesses laughing and jumping with pleasure. At last the eldest said, "Be quick, my sisters, our partners will be impatient." At the end of an hour, when the Star Gazer heard no more noise, he peeped out and saw the twelve sisters in splendid garments, with their satin shoes on their feet, and in their hands the bouquets he had brought them.

"Are you ready?" asked the eldest.

"Yes," replied the other eleven in chorus, and they took their places one by one behind her.

Then the eldest Princess clapped her hands three times and a trap door opened. All the Princesses disappeared down a secret staircase, and Michael hastily followed them.

As he was following in the steps of the Princess Lina, he carelessly trod on her dress.

"There is somebody behind me," cried the Princess; "they are holding my dress."

He Hid Himself Under One of the Beds.

"You foolish thing," said her eldest sister, "you are always afraid of something. It is only a nail which caught you."

They went down, down, down, till at last they came to a passage with a door at one end, which was only fastened with a latch. The eldest Princess opened it, and they found themselves immediately in a lovely little wood, where the leaves were spangled with drops of silver which shone in the brilliant light of the moon.

They next crossed another wood where the leaves were sprinkled with gold, and after that another still, where the leaves glittered with diamonds.

At last the Star Gazer perceived a large lake, and on the shores of the lake twelve little boats with awnings, in which were seated twelve Princes who, grasping their oars, awaited the Princesses.

Each Princess entered one of the boats, and Michael slipped into that which held the youngest. The boats glided along rapidly, but Lina's, from being heavier, was always behind the rest. "We never went so slowly before," said the Princess; "what can be the reason?"

"I don't know," answered the Prince. "I assure you I am rowing as hard as I can."

On the other side of the lake Michael saw a beautiful castle splendidly illuminated, whence came the lively music of fiddles, kettle drums, and trumpets.

In a moment they touched land, and the company jumped out of the boats; and the Princes, after having securely fastened

Where the Leaves Glittered with Diamonds

them, gave their arms to the Princesses and conducted them to the castle.

Michael followed, and entered the ball-room in their train. Everywhere were mirrors, lights, flowers, and damask hangings.

The Star Gazer was quite bewildered at the magnificence of the sight. He placed himself out of the way in a corner, admiring the grace and beauty of the Princesses. Their loveliness was of every kind. Some were fair and some were dark; some had chestnut hair, or curls darker still, and some had golden locks. Never were so many beautiful Princesses seen together at one time, but the one whom he thought the most beautiful and the most fascinating was the little Princess with the velvet eyes.

With what eagerness she danced! Leaning on her partner's shoulder, she swept by like a whirlwind. Her cheeks flushed, her eyes sparkled, and it was plain that she loved dancing better than anything else.

The poor boy envied those handsome young men with whom she danced so gracefully, but he did not know how little reason he had to be jealous of them.

The young men were really the Princes who, to the number of fifty at least, had tried to steal the Princesses' secret. The Princesses had made them drink something which froze the heart and left nothing but the love of dancing.

They danced on till the shoes of the Princesses were worn with holes. When the cock crowed the third time the fiddles

She Swept by Like a Whirlwind.

stopped, and a delicious supper was served by page boys, consisting of sugared orange flowers, crystallized rose leaves, powdered violets, wafers, and other such, which are, as everyone knows, the favorite food of Princesses.

After supper, the dancers all went back to their boats, and this time the Star Gazer entered that of the eldest Princess. They crossed again the wood with the diamond-spangled leaves, the wood with gold-sprinkled leaves, and the wood whose leaves glittered with drops of silver, and as a proof of what he had seen, the boy broke a small branch from a tree in the last wood. Lina turned as she heard the noise made by the breaking of the branch.

"What was that noise?" she said.

"It was nothing," replied her eldest sister; "it was only the screech of the barn-owl that roosts in one of the turrets of the castle."

While she was speaking Michael managed to slip in front, and running up the staircase, he reached the Princesses' room first. He flung open the window, and sliding down the vine which climbed up the wall, found himself in the garden just as the sun was beginning to rise, and it was time for him to set to his work.

That day, when he made up the bouquets, Michael hid the branch with the silver drops in the nosegay intended for the youngest Princess.

When Lina discovered it she was much surprised. However, she said nothing to her sisters, but as she met Michael by accident

A Small Branch as Proof

while she was walking under the shade of the elms, she suddenly stopped as if to speak to him; then, altering her mind, went on her way.

The same evening the twelve sisters went again to the ball, and the Star Gazer again followed them and crossed the lake in Lina's boat. This time it was the Prince who complained that the boat seemed very heavy.

"It is the heat," replied the Princess. "I, too, have been feeling very warm."

During the ball she looked everywhere for the gardener's boy, but she never saw him.

As they came back, Michael gathered a branch from the wood with the gold-spangled leaves, and now it was the eldest Princess who heard the noise that it made in breaking.

"It is nothing," said Lina; "only the cry of the owl which roosts in the turrets of the castle."

When Lina awoke the next day, she found the branch in her bouquet. When the sisters went down she stayed a little behind and said to the cow-boy: "Where does this branch come from?"

"Your Royal Highness knows well enough," answered Michael.

"So you have followed us?"

"Yes, Princess."

"How did you manage it? We never saw you."

"I hid myself," replied the Star Gazer quietly.

Princess Lina Looked Everywhere.

The Princess was silent a moment, and then said:

"You know our secret — keep it! Here is the reward for your discretion." And she flung the boy a purse of gold.

"I do not sell my silence," answered Michael, and he went away without picking up the purse.

For three nights Lina neither saw nor heard anything extraordinary; on the fourth she heard a rustling among the diamond spangled leaves of the wood. That day there was a branch from those trees in her bouquet.

She took the Star Gazer aside, and said to him in a harsh voice:

"You know what price my father has promised to pay for our secret?"

"I know, Princess," answered Michael.

"Don't you mean to tell him?"

"That is not my intention."

"Are you afraid?"

"No, Princess."

"What makes you so discreet, then?"

But Michael was silent.

Lina's sisters had seen her talking to the little garden boy, and jeered at her for it.

"What prevents your marrying him?" asked the eldest. "You could become a gardener, too; it is a charming profession. You could live in a cottage at the end of the park, and help your husband

"I Do Not Sell My Silence."

to draw up water from the well, and when we get up you could bring us our bouquets."

The Princess Lina was very angry, and when the Star Gazer presented her bouquet, she received it in a disdainful manner.

Michael behaved most respectfully. He never raised his eyes to her, but nearly all day she felt him at her side without ever seeing him.

One day she made up her mind to tell everything to her eldest sister.

"What!" said she, "this rogue knows our secret, and you never told me! I must lose no time in getting rid of him."

"But how?"

"Why, by having him taken to the tower with the dungeons, of course."

For this was the way that in old times beautiful Princesses got rid of people who knew too much.

But the astonishing part of it was that the youngest sister did not seem at all to relish this method of stopping the mouth of the gardener's boy, who, after all, had said nothing to their father.

It was agreed that the question should be submitted to the other ten sisters. All were on the side of the eldest. Then the youngest sister declared that if they laid a finger on the little garden boy, she would herself go and tell their father the secret of the holes in their shoes.

At last it was decided that he should be put to the test; that

"Taken to the Tower with the Dungeons!"

they would take him to the ball, and at the end of supper would give him the potion which was to enchant him like the rest.

They sent for the Star Gazer, and asked him how he had contrived to learn their secret; but still he remained silent.

Then, in a commanding tone, the eldest sister gave him the order they had agreed upon.

He only answered:

"I will obey."

He had really been present, invisible, at the council of Princesses, and had heard all; but he had made up his mind to drink of the potion, and sacrifice himself to the happiness of the one he loved.

Not wishing, however, to cut a poor figure at the ball by the side of the other dancers, he went at once to the laurels and said:

"My lovely rose laurel, with the golden rake I have raked thee, with the golden bucket I have watered thee, with the silken towel I have dried thee. Dress me like a Prince."

A beautiful pink flower appeared. Michael gathered it, and found himself in a moment clothed in velvet, which was as black as the eyes of the little Princess, with a cap to match, a diamond button, and a blossom of the rose laurel in his button-hole.

Thus dressed, he presented himself that evening before the Duke of Belloy, and obtained leave to try and discover his daughters' secret. He looked so distinguished that hardly anyone would have known who he was.

The Eldest Sister Gave Him the Order.

The twelve Princesses went upstairs to bed. Michael followed them, and waited behind the open door till they gave the signal for departure.

This time he did not cross in Lina's boat. He gave his arm to the eldest sister, danced with each in turn, and was so graceful that everyone was delighted with him. At last the time came for him to dance with the little Princess. She found him the best partner in the world, but he did not dare to speak a single word to her.

When he was taking her back to her place she said to him in a mocking voice:

"Here you are at the summit of your wishes: you are being treated like a Prince."

"Don't be afraid," replied the Star Gazer gently. "You shall never be a gardener's wife."

The little Princess stared at him with a frightened face, and he left her without waiting for an answer.

When the satin slippers were worn through, the fiddles stopped, and the page boys set the table. Michael was placed next to the eldest sister, and opposite to the youngest.

They gave him the most exquisite dishes to eat, and the most delicate wines to drink; and in order to turn his head more completely, compliments and flattery were heaped on him from every side.

But he took care not to be intoxicated, either by the wine or the compliments.

He Danced with Each in Turn.

At last the eldest sister made a sign, as one of the pages brought in a large golden cup.

"The enchanted castle has no more secrets from you," she said to the Star Gazer. "Let us drink to your triumph."

He cast a lingering glance at the little Princess, and without hesitation lifted the cup.

"Don't drink!" cried out the little Princess; "I would rather marry a gardener."

And she burst into tears.

Michael flung the contents of the cup behind him, sprang over the table, and fell at Lina's feet. The rest of the Princes fell likewise at the knees of the Princesses, each of whom chose a husband and raised him to her side. The charm was broken.

The twelve couples embarked in the boats, which crossed back many times in order to carry over the other Princes. Then they all went through the three woods, and when they had passed the door of the underground passage a great noise was heard, as if the enchanted castle was crumbling to the earth.

They went straight to the room of the Duke of Belloy, who had just awoke. Michael held in his hand the golden cup, and he revealed the secret of the holes in the shoes.

"Choose, then," said the Duke, "whichever you prefer."

"My choice is already made," replied the garden boy, and he offered his hand to the youngest Princess, who blushed and lowered her eyes.

"I Would Rather Marry a Gardener!"

Princess Lina did not become a gardener's wife; on the contrary, it was the Star Gazer who became a Prince: but before the marriage ceremony the Princess insisted that he should tell her how he came to discover the secret.

So he showed her the two laurels which had helped him, and she, like a prudent girl, thinking they gave him too much advantage over his wife, cut them off at the root and threw them in the fire.

And this is why the country girls go about singing:

"Into the woods we needn't go,
The laurel trees no longer grow,"

and dance in summer by the light of the moon.

The Star Gazer Became a Prince.

Beautiful Golden Apples

THE · GOLDEN · MERMAID

From the Brothers Grimm

A powerful King had, among many other treasures, a wonderful tree in his garden, which bore every year beautiful golden apples. But the King was never able to enjoy his treasure, for watch and guard them as he would, as soon as they began to get ripe they were always stolen.

At last, in despair, he sent for his three sons, and said to the two eldest, "Get yourselves ready for a journey. Take gold and silver with you, and a large retinue of servants, as beseems two noble princes, and go through the world till you find out who it is that steals my golden apples, and, if possible, bring the thief to me that I may punish him as he deserves."

His sons were delighted at this proposal, for they had long wished to see something of the world, so they got ready for their journey with all haste, bade their father farewell, and left the town.

The youngest Prince was much disappointed that he too was

not sent out on his travels; but his father wouldn't hear of his going, for he had always been looked upon as the stupid one of the family, and the King was afraid of something happening to him. But the Prince begged and implored so long, that at last his father consented to let him go, and furnished him with gold and silver as he had done the Prince's brothers.

But he gave him the most wretched horse in his stable, because the foolish youth hadn't asked for a better. So the youngest Prince set out on his journey to secure the thief amid the jeers and laughter of the whole court and town.

His path led him first through a wood, and he hadn't gone very far when he met a lean-looking wolf who stood still as he approached. The Prince asked him if he were hungry, and when the wolf said he was, the Prince got down from his horse and said, "If you are really as you say and look, you may take my horse and end it."

The wolf didn't wait to have the offer repeated, but set to work, and soon made an end of the poor beast. When the Prince saw how different the wolf looked when he had finished his meal, he said to him, "Now, my friend, since you have eaten up my horse, and I have such a long way to go that with the best will in the world, I couldn't manage it on foot, the least you can do for me is to act as my horse and to take me on your back."

"Most certainly," said the wolf, and, letting the Prince mount him, he trotted gaily through the wood. After they had gone a lit-

"Take Me on Your Back."

tle way he turned round and asked his rider where he wanted to go, and the Prince proceeded to tell him the whole story of the golden apples that had been stolen out of the King's garden, and how his two brothers had set forth with many followers to find the thief.

When he had finished his story, the wolf, who was in reality no wolf but a mighty magician, said he thought he could tell him who the thief was, and could help to secure him.

"There lives," he said, "in a neighboring country, a mighty Emperor who has a beautiful golden bird in a cage, and this is the creature who steals the golden apples, but it flies so fast that it is impossible to catch at its theft. You must slip into the Emperor's palace by night and steal the bird with the cage; but be very careful not to touch the walls as you go out."

The following night the Prince stole into the Emperor's palace, and found the bird in its cage as the wolf had told him he would. He took hold of it carefully, but in spite of all his caution he touched the wall in trying to pass by some sleeping watchmen. They awoke at once, and, seizing him, beat him and put him into chains. The next day he was led before the Emperor, who at once condemned him to death and to be thrown into a dark dungeon till the day of his execution arrived.

The wolf, who of course knew by his magic arts all that had happened to the Prince, turned himself at once into a mighty King with a large train of followers, and proceeded to the court of the Emperor, where he was received with every show of honor. The

"This is the Creature Who Steals the Golden Apples."

Emperor and he conversed on many subjects, and, among other things, the stranger asked his host if he had many prisoners.

The Emperor told him he had more than he knew what to do with, and that a new one had been captured that very night for trying to steal his magic bird, but that as he had already more than enough to feed and support, he was going to have this last captive hanged the next morning.

"He must have been a most daring thief," said the King, "to try and steal the magic bird, for depend upon it the creature must have been well guarded. I would really like to see this bold rascal."

"By all means," said the Emperor; and he himself led his guest down to the dungeon where the unfortunate Prince was kept prisoner.

When the Emperor stepped out of the cell with the King, the latter turned to him and said, "Most mighty Emperor, I have been much disappointed. I had thought to find a powerful robber, and instead of that I have seen the most miserable creature I can imagine. Hanging is far too good for him. If I had to sentence him I should make him perform some very difficult task, under pain of death. If he did it so much the better for you, and if he didn't, matters would just be as they are now and he could still be hanged."

"Your counsel," said the Emperor, "is excellent, and, as it happens, I've got the very thing for him to do. My nearest neighbor, who is also a mighty Emperor, possesses a golden horse which

"I Would Like to See This Bold Rascal."

he guards most carefully. The prisoner shall be told to steal this horse and bring it to me."

The Prince was then let out of his dungeon, and told his life would be spared if he succeeded in bringing the golden horse to the Emperor. He did not feel very elated at this announcement, for he did not know how in the world he was to set about the task, and he started on his way weeping bitterly, and wondering what had made him leave his father's house and kingdom.

But before he had gone far his friend, the wolf, stood before him and said, "Dear Prince, why are you so cast down? It is true you didn't succeed in catching the bird; but don't let that discourage you, for this time you will be all the more careful, and will doubtless catch the horse."

With these and like words the wolf comforted the Prince, and warned him specially not to touch the wall or let the horse touch it as he led it out, or he would fail in the same way as he had done with the bird.

After a somewhat lengthy journey, the Prince and the wolf came to the kingdom ruled over by the Emperor who possessed the golden horse. Late one evening they reached the capital, and the wolf advised the Prince to set to work at once, before their presence in the city had aroused the watchfulness of the guards. They slipped unnoticed into the Emperor's stables and into the very place where there were the most guards, for there the wolf rightly surmised they would find the horse.

His Life Would be Spared.

When they came to a certain inner door the wolf told the Prince to remain outside, while he went in. In a short time he returned and said, "My dear Prince, the horse is most securely watched, but I have bewitched all the guards, and if you will only be careful not to touch the wall yourself, or let the horse touch it as you go out, there is no danger and the game is yours."

The Prince, who had made up his mind to be more than cautious this time, went cheerfully to work. He found all the guards fast asleep, and, slipping into the horse's stall, he seized it by the bridle and led it out; but, unfortunately, before they had got quite clear of the stables a gadfly stung the horse and caused it to swish its tail, whereby it touched the wall.

In a moment all the guards awoke, seized the Prince and beat him mercilessly with their horse-whips, after which they bound him with chains, and flung him into a dungeon.

The next morning they brought him before the Emperor, who treated him exactly as the King with the golden bird had done, and commanded him to be beheaded on the following day.

When the wolf-magician saw that the Prince had failed this time, too, he transformed himself again into a mighty King, and proceeded with an even more gorgeous retinue than the first time to the court of this Emperor. He was courteously received and entertained, and once more after dinner he led the conversation to the subject of prisoners, and in the course of it again requested to be allowed to see the bold robber who had dared to break

The Guards Seized the Prince.

into the Emperor's stable to steal his most valuable possession.

The Emperor consented, and all happened exactly as it had at the court of the Emperor with the golden bird; the prisoner's life was to be spared only on condition that within three days he should obtain possession of the golden mermaid, whom hitherto no mortal had ever approached.

Very depressed by his dangerous and difficult task, the Prince left his gloomy prison; but, to his great joy, he met his friend the wolf before he had gone many miles on his journey. At first, the cunning creature pretended he knew nothing of what had happened to the Prince, and asked him how he had fared with the horse. The Prince told him all about his misadventure, and the condition on which the Emperor had promised to spare his life.

Then the wolf revealed to him that he had twice got the Prince out of prison, and that if he would only trust in him, and do exactly as he told him, he would certainly succeed in this last undertaking.

Thereupon they bent their steps towards the sea, which stretched out before them, as far as their eyes could see, all the waves dancing and glittering in the bright sunshine.

"Now," continued the wolf, "I am going to turn myself into a boat full of the most beautiful silken merchandise, and you must jump boldly into the boat, and steer with my tail in your hand right out into the open sea. You will soon come upon the golden mermaid. Whatever you do, don't follow her if she calls you, but on the contrary say to her, 'The buyer comes to the seller, not the

They Bent Their Steps Towards the Sea.

seller to the buyer.' After which you must steer towards the land, and she will follow you, for she won't be able to resist the beautiful wares you have on board your ship."

The Prince promised faithfully to do all he had been told, whereupon the wolf changed himself into a ship full of the most exquisite silks, of every shade and color imaginable. The astonished Prince stepped into the boat, and, holding the wolf's tail in his hand, he steered boldly out into the open sea, where the sun was gilding the blue waves with its golden rays.

Soon he saw the golden mermaid swimming near the ship, beckoning and calling to him to follow her; but, mindful of the wolf's warning, he told her in a loud voice that if she wished to buy anything she must come to him.

With these words he turned his magic ship round and steered back towards the land. The mermaid called out to him to stand still, but he refused to listen to her and never paused till he reached the sand of the shore. Here he stopped and waited for the mermaid, who had swum after him.

When she drew near the boat he saw that she was far more beautiful than any mortal he had ever beheld. She swam round the ship for some time, and then swung herself gracefully on board, in order to examine the beautiful silken stuffs more closely.

Then the Prince seized her in his arms, and kissing her tenderly on the cheeks and lips, he told her she was his for ever; at the same moment the boat turned into a wolf again, which so terrified

He Saw the Golden Mermaid.

the mermaid that she clung to the Prince for protection.

So the golden mermaid was successfully caught, and she soon felt quite happy in her new life when she saw she had nothing to fear either from the Prince or the wolf — she rode on the back of the latter, and the Prince rode behind her.

When they reached the country ruled over by the Emperor with the golden horse, the Prince jumped down, and, helping the mermaid to alight, he led her before the Emperor. At the sight of the beautiful mermaid and of the grim wolf, who stuck close to the Prince this time, the guards all made respectful obeisance, and soon the three stood before his Imperial Majesty. When the Emperor heard from the Prince how he had gained possession of his fair prize, he at once recognized that he had been helped by some magic art, and on the spot gave up all claim to the beautiful mermaid.

"Dear youth," he said, "forgive me for my shameful conduct to you, and, as a sign that you pardon me, accept the golden horse as a present. I acknowledge your power to be greater even than I can understand, for you have succeeded in gaining possession of the golden mermaid, whom hitherto no mortal has ever been able to approach."

Then they all sat down to a huge feast, and the Prince had to relate his adventures all over again, to the wonder and astonishment of the whole company.

But the Prince was wearying now to return to his own king-

The Three Stood Before His Imperial Majesty.

dom, so as soon as the feast was over he took farewell of the Emperor, and set out on his homeward way. He lifted the mermaid on to the golden horse, and swung himself up behind her — and so they rode on merrily, with the wolf trotting behind, till they came to the country of the Emperor with the golden bird.

The renown of the Prince and his adventure had gone before him, and the Emperor sat on his throne awaiting the arrival of the Prince and his companions. When the three rode into the courtyard of the palace, they were surprised and delighted to find everything festively illuminated and decorated for their reception. Then the Prince and the golden mermaid, with the wolf behind them, mounted the steps of the palace; the Emperor came forward to meet them, and led them to the throne room.

At the same moment a servant appeared with the golden bird in its golden cage, and the Emperor begged the Prince to accept it with his love, and to forgive him the indignity he had suffered at his hands.

Then the Emperor bent low before the beautiful mermaid, and, offering her his arm, he led her into dinner, closely followed by the Prince and their friend the wolf; the latter seating himself at table, not the least embarrassed that no one had invited him to do so.

As soon as the sumptuous meal was over, the Prince and his mermaid took leave of the Emperor, and, seating themselves on the golden horse, continued their homeward journey. On the way

He Lifted the Mermaid Onto the Golden Horse.

the wolf turned to the Prince and said, "Dear friends, I must now bid you farewell, but I leave you under such happy circumstances that I cannot feel our parting to be a sad one."

The Prince was very unhappy when he heard these words, and begged the wolf to stay with them always; but this the good creature refused to do, though he thanked the Prince kindly for his invitation, and called out as he disappeared into the thicket, "Should any evil befall you, dear Prince, at any time, you may rely on my friendship and gratitude."

These were the wolf's parting words, and the Prince could not restrain his tears when he saw his friend vanishing in the distance; but one glance at his beloved mermaid soon cheered him up again, and they continued on their journey merrily.

The news of his son's adventures had already reached his father's court, and everyone was more than astonished at the success of the once-mocked Prince. His elder brothers, who had in vain gone in pursuit of the thief of the golden apples, were furious over their younger brother's good fortune, and plotted and planned how to kill him.

They hid themselves in the wood through which the Prince had to pass on his way to the palace, and there fell on him, and, having beaten him to death, they carried off the golden horse and the golden bird.

But nothing they could do would persuade the golden mermaid to go with them or move from the spot, for ever since she

"Should Any Evil Befall You . . ."

had left the sea, she had so attached herself to her Prince that she asked nothing else than to live or die with him.

For many weeks the poor mermaid sat and watched over the dead body of her lover, weeping salt tears over his loss, when suddenly one day their old friend the wolf appeared and said, "Cover the Prince's body with all the leaves and flowers you can find in the wood."

The maiden did as he told her, and then the wolf breathed over the flowery grave, and, lo and behold! The Prince lay there sleeping as peacefully as a child.

"Now you may wake him if you like," said the wolf, and the mermaid bent over him and gently kissed the wounds his brothers had made on his forehead, and the Prince awoke, and you may imagine how delighted he was to find his beautiful mermaid beside him, though he felt a little depressed when he thought of the loss of the golden bird and the golden horse.

After a time the wolf, who had likewise fallen on the Prince's neck, advised them to continue their journey, and once more the Prince and his lovely bride mounted on the faithful beast's back.

The King's joy was great when he embraced his youngest son, for he had long since despaired of his return. He received the wolf and the beautiful golden mermaid most cordially, too, and the Prince was made to tell his adventures all over from the beginning.

The poor old father grew very sad when he heard of the shameful conduct of his elder sons, and had them called before him.

The Mermaid Wept Salt Tears.

THE GOLDEN MERMAID

They turned as white as death when they saw their brother, whom they thought they had murdered, standing beside them alive and well, and so startled were they that when the King asked them why they had behaved so wickedly to their brother they could think of no lie, but confessed at once that they had slain the young Prince in order to obtain possession of the golden horse and the golden bird.

Their father's wrath knew no bounds, and he ordered them both to be banished, but he could not do enough to honor his youngest son, and his marriage with the beautiful mermaid was celebrated with much pomp and magnificence. When the festivities were over, the wolf bade them all farewell, and returned once more to his life in the woods, much to the regret of the old King, the young Prince, and his bride.

And so ended the adventures of the Prince with his friend the wolf.

Both to be Banished

The Pot of Pinks to Console Her.

FELICIA · AND · THE · PRETTY · PINKS

O nce upon a time there was a poor laborer who, feeling that he had not much longer to live, wished to divide his possessions between his son and daughter, whom he loved dearly.

So he called them to him, and said: "Your mother brought me as her dowry two stools and a straw bed; I have, besides, a hen, a flowerpot of pinks, and a silver ring, which were given me by a noble lady who once lodged in my poor cottage. When she went away she said to me:

'Be careful of my gifts, good man; see that you do not lose the ring or forget to water the pinks. As for your daughter, I promise you that she shall be more beautiful than anyone you ever saw in your life; call her Felicia, and when she grows up give her the ring and the pot of pinks to console her for her poverty.' Take them both then, my dear child," he added, "and your brother shall have everything else."

The two children seemed quite contented, and when their

father died they wept for him, and divided his possessions as he had told them. Felicia believed that her brother loved her, but when she sat down upon one of the stools he said angrily:

"Keep your pot of pinks and your ring, but let my things alone. I like order in my house."

Felicia, who was very gentle, said nothing, but stood up crying quietly; while Bruno, for that was her brother's name, sat comfortably by the fire. Presently, when supper-time came, Bruno had a delicious egg, and he threw the shell to Felicia, saying:

"There, that is all I can give you; if you don't like it, go out and catch frogs; there are plenty of them in the marsh close by."

Felicia did not answer, but she cried more bitterly than ever, and went away to her own little room. She found it filled with the sweet scent of the flowers, and, going up to them, she said sadly: "Beautiful pinks, you are so sweet and so pretty, you are the only comfort I have left. Be very sure that I will take care of you, and water you well, and never allow any cruel hand to tear you from your stems."

As she leant over them she noticed that they were very dry. So taking her pitcher, she ran off in the clear moonlight to the fountain, which was at some distance. When she reached it she sat down upon the brink to rest, but she had hardly done so when she saw a stately lady coming towards her, surrounded by numbers of attendants. Six maids of honor carried her train, and she leaned upon the arm of another.

Six Maids Carried Her Train.

When they came near the fountain a canopy was spread for her, under which was placed a sofa of cloth-of-gold, and presently a dainty supper was served, upon a table covered with dishes of gold and crystal, while the wind in the trees and the falling water of the fountain murmured the softest music.

Felicia was hidden in the shade, too much astonished by all she saw to venture to move; but in a few moments the Queen said:

"I fancy I see a shepherdess near that tree; bid her come hither."

So Felicia came forward and saluted the Queen timidly, but with so much grace that all were surprised.

"What are you doing here, my pretty child?" asked the Queen. "Are you not afraid of robbers?"

"Ah! Madam," said Felicia, "a poor shepherdess who has nothing to lose does not fear robbers."

"You are not very rich, then?" said the Queen, smiling.

"I am so poor," answered Felicia, "that a pot of pinks and a silver ring are my only possessions in all the world."

"But you have a heart," said the Queen. "What should you say if anybody wanted to steal that?"

"I do not know what it is like to lose one's heart, madam," she replied; "but I have always heard that without a heart one cannot live, and if it is broken one must die; and in spite of my poverty I should be sorry not to live."

"You are quite right to take care of your heart, pretty one," said the Queen. "But tell me, have you supped?"

Felicia Came Forward.

"No, madam," answered Felicia; "my brother ate all the supper there was."

Then the Queen ordered that a place should be made for her at the table, and herself loaded Felicia's plate with good things, but Felicia was too much astonished to be hungry.

"I want to know what you were doing at the fountain so late," said the Queen presently.

"I came to fetch a pitcher of water for my pinks, madam," she answered, stooping to pick up the pitcher which stood beside her; but when she showed it to the Queen she was amazed to see that it had turned to gold, all sparkling with great diamonds, and the water, of which it was full, was more fragrant than the sweetest roses. She was afraid to take it until the Queen said:

"It is yours, Felicia; go and water your pinks with it, and let it remind you that the Queen of the Woods is your friend."

The shepherdess threw herself at the Queen's feet, and thanked her humbly for her gracious words.

"Ah! Madam," she cried, "if I might beg you to stay here a moment I would run and fetch my pot of pinks for you — they could not fall into better hands."

"Go, Felicia," said the Queen, stroking her cheek softly; "I will wait here until you come back."

So Felicia took up her pitcher and ran to her little room, but while she had been away Bruno had gone in and taken the pot of pinks, leaving a great cabbage in its place. When she saw the un-

It Had Turned to Gold.

lucky cabbage Felicia was much distressed, and did not know what to do; but at last she ran back to the fountain, and, kneeling before the Queen, said:

"Madam, Bruno has stolen my pot of pinks, so I have nothing but my silver ring; I beg you to accept it as proof of my gratitude."

"But if I take your ring, my pretty shepherdess," said the Queen, "you will have nothing left, and what will you do then?"

"Ah! Madam," she answered simply, "if I have your friendship I shall do very well."

So the Queen took the ring and put it on her finger, and mounted her chariot, which was made of coral studded with emeralds, and drawn by six milk-white horses. And Felicia looked after her until the winding of the forest path hid her from her sight, and then she went back to the cottage, thinking over all the wonderful things that had happened.

The first thing she did when she reached her room was to throw the cabbage out of the window.

But she was very much surprised to hear an odd little voice cry out: "Oh! I am half killed!" and could not tell where it came from, because cabbages do not generally speak.

As soon as it was light, Felicia, who was very unhappy about her pot of pinks, went out to look for it, and the first thing she found was the unfortunate cabbage. She gave it a push with her foot, saying: "What are you doing here, and how dared you put

"I Beg You to Accept It."

yourself in the place of my pot of pinks?"

"If I hadn't been carried," replied the cabbage, "you may be very sure that I shouldn't have thought of going there."

It made her shiver with fright to hear the cabbage talk, but he went on:

"If you will be good enough to plant me by my comrades again, I can tell you where your pinks are at this moment — hidden in Bruno's bed!"

Felicia was in despair when she heard this, not knowing how she was to get them back. But she replanted the cabbage very kindly in his old place, and, as she finished doing it, she saw Bruno's hen, and said, catching hold of it:

"Come here, horrid little creature! You shall suffer for all the unkind things my brother has done to me."

"Ah! Shepherdess," said the hen, "don't kill me; I am rather a gossip, and I can tell you some surprising things that you will like to hear. Don't imagine that you are the daughter of the poor laborer who brought you up; your mother was a Queen who had six girls already, and the King threatened that unless she had a son who could inherit his kingdom she should have her head cut off.

"So when the Queen had another little daughter she was quite frightened, and agreed with her sister (who was a Fairy) to exchange her for the Fairy's little son. Now the Queen had been shut up in a great tower by the King's orders, and when a great many days went by and still she heard nothing from the Fairy, she

It Made Her Shiver to Hear the Cabbage Talk.

made her escape from the window by means of a rope ladder, taking her little baby with her.

"After wandering about until she was half dead with cold and fatigue she reached this cottage. I was the laborer's wife, and was a good nurse, and the Queen gave you into my charge, and told me all her misfortunes, and then died before she had time to say what was to become of you.

"As I never in all my life could keep a secret, I could not help telling this strange tale to my neighbors, and one day a beautiful lady came here, and I told it to her also. When I had finished she touched me with a wand she held in her hand, and instantly I became a hen, and there was an end of my talking!

"I was very sad, and my husband, who was out when it happened, never knew what had become of me. After seeking me everywhere he believed that I must have been drowned, or eaten up by wild beasts in the forest.

"That same lady came here once more, and commanded that you should be called Felicia, and left the ring and the pot of pinks to be given to you, and while she was in the house twenty-five of the King's guards came to search for you, doubtless meaning to kill you, but she muttered a few words, and immediately they all turned into cabbages. It was one of them whom you threw out of your window yesterday.

"I don't know how it was that he could speak — I have never heard either of them say a word before, nor have I been able to

"Taking Her Little Baby with Her."

do it myself until now."

The Princess was greatly astonished at the hen's story, and said kindly: "I am truly sorry for you, my poor nurse, and wish it was in my power to restore you to your real form. But we must not despair; it seems to me, after what you have told me, that something must be going to happen soon. Just now, however, I must go and look for my pinks, which I love better than anything in the world."

Bruno had gone out into the forest, never thinking that Felicia would search in his room for the pinks, and she was delighted by his unexpected absence, and thought to get them back without further trouble. But as soon as she entered the room she saw a terrible army of rats, who were guarding the straw bed; and when she attempted to approach it they sprang at her, biting and scratching furiously. Quite terrified, she drew back, crying out: "Oh! My dear pinks, how can you stay here in such bad company?"

Then she suddenly bethought herself of the pitcher of water, and, hoping that it might have some magic power, she ran to fetch it, and sprinkled a few drops over the fierce-looking swarm of rats. In a moment not a tail nor a whisker was to be seen. Each one had made for his hole as fast as his legs could carry him, so that the Princess could safely take her pot of pinks.

She found them nearly dying for want of water, and hastily poured all that was left in the pitcher upon them. As she bent over them, enjoying their delicious scent, a soft voice, that seemed to rustle among the leaves, said:

Astonished at the Hen's Story

"Lovely Felicia, the day has come at last when I may have the happiness of telling you how even the flowers love you and rejoice in your beauty."

The Princess, quite overcome by the strangeness of hearing a cabbage, a hen, and a pink speak, and by the terrible sight of an army of rats, suddenly became very pale, and fainted away.

At this moment in came Bruno. Working hard in the heat had not improved his temper, and when he saw that Felicia had succeeded in finding her pinks, he was so angry that he dragged her out into the garden and shut the door upon her. The fresh air soon made her open her pretty eyes, and there before her stood the Queen of the Woods, looking as charming as ever.

"You have a bad brother," she said; "I saw how cruelly he turned you out. Shall I punish him for it?"

"Ah! No, madam," she said; "I am not angry with him."

"But supposing he was not your brother, after all, what would you say then?" asked the Queen.

"Oh! But I think he must be," said Felicia.

"What!" said the Queen, "have you not heard that you are a Princess?"

"I was told so a little while ago, madam, but how could I believe it without a single proof?"

"Ah! Dear child," said the Queen, "the way you speak assures me that, in spite of your humble upbringing, you are indeed a real Princess, and I can save you from being treated in such a way again."

"Even the Flowers Love You."

She was interrupted at this moment by the arrival of a very handsome young man. He wore a coat of green velvet fastened with emerald clasps, and had a crown of pinks on his head. He knelt upon one knee and kissed the Queen's hand.

"Ah!" she cried, "My pink, my dear son, what a happiness to see you restored to your natural shape by Felicia's aid!" And she embraced him joyfully. Then turning to Felicia she said:

"Charming Princess, I know all the hen told you, but you cannot have heard that the zephyrs, to whom was entrusted the task of carrying my son to the tower where the Queen, your mother, so anxiously waited for him, left him instead in a garden of flowers, while they flew off to tell your mother. Whereupon a fairy with whom I had quarreled changed him into a pink, and I could do nothing to prevent it.

"You may imagine how angry I was, and how I tried to find some means of undoing the mischief she had done; but there was no help for it. I could only bring the Prince to the place where you were being brought up, hoping that when you grew up he might love you, and by your care be restored to his natural form. And you see everything has come right as I hoped it would. Your giving me the silver ring was the sign that the power of the charm was nearly over, and my enemy's last chance was to frighten you with her army of rats. That she did not succeed in doing; so now, my dear Felicia, if you will be married to my son with this silver ring, your future happiness is certain. Do you think him handsome

"What Happiness To See You Restored!"

and amiable enough to be willing to marry him?"

Madam," replied Felicia, blushing, "you overwhelm me with your kindness. I know that by your art you turned the soldiers who were sent to kill me into cabbages, and my nurse into a hen, and that you do me only too much honor in proposing that I shall marry your son. How can I explain to you the cause of my hesitation? I feel, for the first time in my life, how happy it would make me to be beloved. Can you indeed give me the Prince's heart?"

"It is yours already, lovely Princess!" he cried, taking her hand in his. "But for the horrible enchantment which kept me silent, I should have told you long ago how dearly I love you."

This made the Princess very happy, and the Queen, who could not bear to see her dressed like a poor shepherdess, touched her with her wand, saying:

"I wish you to be attired as befits your rank and beauty." And immediately the Princess's cotton dress became a magnificent robe of silver brocade embroidered with gems, and her soft dark hair was encircled by a crown of diamonds, from which floated a clear white veil. With her bright eyes, and the charming color in her cheeks, she was altogether such a dazzling sight that the Prince could hardly bear it.

"How pretty you are, Felicia!" he cried. "Don't keep me in suspense, I entreat you; say that you will marry me."

"Ah!" said the Queen, smiling, "I think she will not refuse now."

"As Befits Your Rank and Beauty"

Just then Bruno, who was going back to his work, came out of the cottage, and thought he must be dreaming when he saw Felicia; but she called him very kindly, and begged the Queen to take pity on him.

"What!" she said, "when he was so unkind to you?"

"Ah! Madam," said the Princess, "I am so happy that I should like everybody else to be happy, too."

The Queen kissed her, and said: "Well, to please you, let me see what I can do for this cross Bruno." And with a wave of her wand she turned the poor little cottage into a splendid palace, full of treasures; only the two stools and the straw bed remained just as they were, to remind him of his former poverty.

Then the Queen touched Bruno himself, and made him gentle and polite and grateful, and he thanked her and the Princess a thousand times. Lastly, the Queen restored the hen and the cabbages to their natural forms, and left them all very contented.

The Prince and Princess were married as soon as possible with great splendor, and lived happily ever after.

Bruno Thought He Must be Dreaming.

Snow-White and Rose-Red

Snow-White · and · Rose-Red

From the Brothers Grimm

A poor widow once lived in a little cottage with a garden in front of it, in which grew two rose trees, one bearing white roses and the other red. She had two children, who were just like the two rose trees; one was called Snow-White and the other Rose-Red, and they were the sweetest and best children in the world, always diligent and always cheerful; but Snow-White was quieter and more gentle than Rose-Red.

Rose-Red loved to run about the fields and meadows, and to pick flowers and catch butterflies; but Snow-White sat at home with her mother and helped her in the household, or read aloud to her when there was no work to do.

The two children loved each other so dearly that they always walked about hand in hand whenever they went out together, and when Snow-White said: "We will never desert each other," Rose-Red answered: "No, not as long as we live;" and the mother added: "Whatever one gets she shall share with the other."

They often roamed about in the woods gathering berries and no beast hurt them; on the contrary, they came up to them in the most pleasant manner; the little hare would eat a cabbage leaf from their hands, the deer grazed beside them, the stag would bound past them merrily, and the birds remained on the branches and sang to them with all their might.

No evil ever befell them; if they tarried late in the wood and night overtook them, they lay down on the moss and slept till morning, and their mother knew they were quite safe, and never felt anxious about them.

Once, when they had slept the night in the wood and had been wakened by the morning sun, they perceived a beautiful child in a shining white robe sitting close to their resting-place. The figure got up, looked at them kindly, but said nothing, and vanished into the wood. And when they looked round about them they became aware that they had slept quite close to a precipice, over which they would certainly have fallen had they gone on a few steps further in the darkness. And when they told their mother of their adventure, she said what they had seen must have been the angel that guards good children.

Snow-White and Rose-Red kept their mother's cottage so beautifully clean and neat that it was a pleasure to go into it. In summer Rose-Red looked after the house, and every morning before her mother awoke she placed a bunch of flowers before the bed, and from each tree a rose. In winter Snow-White lit the fire

They Roamed in the Woods.

and put on the kettle, which was made of brass, but so beautifully polished that it shone like gold. In the evening when the snowflakes fell their mother said: "Snow-White, go and close the shutters;" and they drew round the fire, while the mother put on her spectacles and read aloud from a big book and the two girls listened and sat and spun. Beside them on the ground lay a little lamb, and behind them perched a little white dove with its head tucked under its wings.

One evening as they sat thus cozily together someone knocked at the door as though he desired admittance. The mother said: "Rose-Red, open the door quickly; it must be some traveller seeking shelter." Rose-Red hastened to unbar the door, and thought she saw a poor man standing in the darkness outside; but it was no such thing, only a bear, who poked his thick black head through the door. Rose-Red screamed aloud and sprang back in terror, the lamb began to bleat, the dove flapped its wings, and Snow-White ran and hid behind her mother's bed.

But the bear began to speak, and said: "Don't be afraid: I won't hurt you. I am half frozen, and only wish to warm myself a little."

"My poor bear," said the mother, "lie down by the fire, only take care you don't burn your fur." Then she called out: "Snow-White and Rose-Red, come out; the bear will do you no harm: he is a good, honest creature."

So they both came out of their hiding places, and gradually

"Some Traveler Seeking Shelter."

the lamb and dove drew near, too, and they all forgot their fear. The bear asked the children to beat the snow out of his fur, and they fetched a brush and scrubbed him till he was dry. Then the beast stretched himself in front of the fire, and growled quite happily and comfortably.

The children soon grew quite at their ease with him, and led their helpless guest a fearful life. They tugged his fur with their hands, put their small feet on his back, and rolled him about here and there, or took a hazel wand and beat him with it; and if he growled they only laughed.

The bear submitted to everything with the best possible good-nature, only when they went too far he cried: "Oh! children, spare my life!" Then he added:

"Snow-White and Rose-Red,
   Don't beat your lover dead."

When it was time to retire for the night, and the others went to bed, the mother said to the bear: "You can lie there on the hearth, in heaven's name; it will be shelter for you from the cold and wet." As soon as day dawned the children let him out, and he trotted over the snow and into the wood.

From this time on, the bear came every evening at the same hour, and lay down by the hearth and let the children play what pranks they liked with him; and they got so accustomed to him that the door was never shut till their black friend had made his appearance.

They All Forgot Their Fear.

When spring came, and all outside was green, the bear said one morning to Snow-White: "Now I must go away, and not return again the whole summer."

"Where are you going to, dear bear?" asked Snow-White.

"I must go to the wood and protect my treasure from the wicked dwarfs. In winter, when the earth is frozen hard, they are obliged to remain underground, for they can't work their way through; but now, when the sun has thawed and warmed the ground, they break through and come up above to spy the land and steal what they can: what once falls into their hands and into their caves is not easily brought back to light."

Snow-White was quite sad over their friend's departure, and when she unbarred the door for him, the bear, stepping out, caught a piece of his fur in the doorknocker. Snow-White thought she caught sight of glittering gold beneath it, but she couldn't be certain of it; and the bear ran hastily away, and soon disappeared behind the trees.

A short time after this the mother sent the children into the forest to collect wood. They came in their wanderings upon a big tree which lay felled on the ground, and on the trunk among the long grass they noticed something jumping up and down, but what it was they couldn't distinguish.

When they approached nearer they perceived a dwarf with a wrinkly face and a beard a yard long. The end of the beard was jammed into a cleft of the tree, and the little man sprang about like

"Now I Must Go Away."

a dog on a chain, and didn't seem to know what he was to do. He glared at the girls with his fiery red eyes, and screamed out: "What are you standing there for? Can't you come and help me?"

"What were you doing, little man?" asked Rose-Red.

"You stupid, inquisitive goose!" replied the dwarf; "I wanted to split the tree, in order to get little chips of wood for our kitchen fire; those thick logs that serve to make fires for coarse, greedy people like yourselves quite burn up all the little food we need. I had successfully driven in the wedge, and all was going well, but the cursed wood was so slippery that it suddenly sprang out, and the tree closed up so rapidly that I had no time to take my beautiful white beard out, so here I am stuck fast, and I can't get away; and you silly, smooth-faced, milk-and-water girls just stand and laugh! Ugh! What wretches you are!"

The children did all in their power, but they couldn't get the beard out; it was wedged in far too firmly. "I will run and fetch somebody," said Rose-Red.

"Crazy blockheads!" snapped the dwarf; "What's the good of calling anyone else? You're already two too many for me. Does nothing better occur to you than that?"

"Don't be so impatient," said Snow-White, "I'll see you get help;" and taking her scissors out of her pocket she cut the end off his beard.

As soon as the dwarf felt himself free he seized a bag full of gold which was hidden among the roots of the tree, lifted it up,

"You Stupid Inquisitive Goose!"

and muttered aloud: "Curse these rude wretches, cutting off a piece of my splendid beard!" With these words he swung the bag over his back, and disappeared without as much as looking at the children again.

Shortly after this Snow-White and Rose-Red went out to get a dish of fish. As they approached the stream they saw something which looked like an enormous grasshopper, springing towards the water as if it were going to jump in. They ran forward and recognized their old friend the dwarf. "Where are you going to?" asked Rose-Red. "You're surely not going to jump into the water?"

"I'm not such a fool," screamed the dwarf. "Don't you see that cursed fish is trying to drag me in?"

The little man had been sitting on the bank fishing, when unfortunately the wind had entangled his beard in the line; and when immediately afterwards a big fish bit, the feeble little creature had no strength to pull it out; the fish had the upper fin, and dragged the dwarf towards him. He clung on with all his might to every blade of grass, but it didn't help him much; he had to follow every movement of the fish, and was in great danger of being drawn into the water.

The girls came up just at the right moment, held him firm, and did all they could to disentangle his beard from the line, but in vain; beard and line were in a hopeless muddle. Nothing remained but to produce the scissors and cut the beard, by which a small part of it was sacrificed.

He Swung the Bag Over His Back.

When the dwarf perceived what they were about, he yelled to them: "Do you call that manners, you toadstools! To disfigure a fellow's face? It wasn't enough that you shortened my beard before, but you must now needs cut off the best bit of it? I can't appear like this before my own people!" Then he fetched a sack of pearls that lay among the rushes, and without saying another word he dragged it away and disappeared behind a stone.

It happened that soon after this the mother sent the two girls into town to buy needles, thread, laces, and ribbons. Their road led over a heath where huge boulders of rock lay scattered here and there. While trudging along they saw a big bird hovering in the air, circling slowly above them, always descending lower, till at last it settled on a rock not far from them. Immediately afterwards they heard a sharp, piercing cry. They ran forward, and saw with horror that the eagle had pounced on their old friend the dwarf, and was about to carry him off.

The tender-hearted children seized hold of the little man, and struggled so long with the bird that at last he let go of his prey. When the dwarf had recovered from the first shock, he screamed in his screeching voice: "Couldn't you have treated me more carefully? You have torn my thin little coat all to shreds, useless, awkward girls that you are!" Then he took a bag of precious stones and vanished under the rocks into his cave.

The girls were accustomed to his ingratitude, and went on their way and did their business in town. On the way home, as

Their Road Led Over a Heath.

they were again passing the heath, they surprised the dwarf pouring out his precious stones on an open space, for he had thought no one would pass by at so late an hour. The evening sun shone on the glittering stones, and they glanced and gleamed so beautifully that the children stood still and gazed on them.

"What are you standing there gaping for?" screamed the dwarf, and his ashen-grey face became scarlet with rage. He was about to go off with these angry words when a sudden growl was heard, and a black bear trotted out of the wood. The dwarf jumped up in a great fright, but he hadn't time to reach his place of retreat, for the bear was already close to him.

Then he cried in terror: "Dear Mr. Bear, spare me! I'll give you all my treasure. Look at those beautiful precious stones lying there. Spare my life! What pleasure would you get from a poor feeble little fellow like me? You won't feel me between your teeth! There, lay hold of these two wicked girls, they will be tender morsels for you as young quails; eat them up, for heaven's sake."

But the bear, paying no attention to his words, gave the evil little creature one blow with his paw, and he never moved again.

The girls had run away, but the bear called after them: "Snow-White and Rose-Red, don't be afraid; wait, and I'll come with you."

They recognized his voice and stood still, and when the bear was quite close to them his skin suddenly fell off, and a beautiful man stood beside them, all dressed in gold. "I am a King's son," he

The Dwarf Jumped Up in a Great Fright.

said, "and have been doomed by that little dwarf, who had stolen my treasure, to roam about the woods as a wild bear till his death should set me free. Now he has got his well-merited punishment."

Snow-White married him, and Rose-Red his brother, and they divided the great treasure the dwarf had collected in his cave between them. Their mother lived for many years peacefully with her children, and she carried the two rose trees with her. They stood in front of her window, and every year they bore the finest red and white roses.

They Divided the Great Treasure.

The Princess's Horse was Called Falada.

THE · GOOSE-GIRL

From the Brothers Grimm

Once upon a time an old Queen, whose husband had been dead for many years, had a beautiful daughter. When she grew up she was betrothed to a Prince who lived a great way off. Now, when the time drew near for her to be married and to depart into that foreign kingdom, her old mother gave her much costly baggage, and many ornaments, gold and silver, trinkets and knicknacks, and everything that belonged to a royal trousseau, for she loved her daughter very dearly.

The Queen gave her a waiting-maid also, who was to ride with her and hand her over to the bridegroom, and she provided each of them with a horse for the journey. Now the Princess's horse was called Falada, and he could speak.

When the hour for departure drew near, the old mother went to her bedroom, and taking a small knife she cut her finger till it bled; then she held a white rag and let three drops of blood fall into it. She gave it to her daughter, and said: "Dear child, take great care of this rag: it may be of use to you on the journey."

So they took a sad farewell of each other, and the Princess stuck the rag in front of her dress, mounted her horse, and set forth on the journey to her bridegroom's kingdom. After they had ridden for about an hour the Princess began to feel very thirsty, and said to her waiting-maid: "Pray get down and fetch me some water in my golden cup out of yonder stream: I would like a drink."

"If you're thirsty," said the maid, "dismount yourself, and lie down by the water and drink; I don't mean to be your servant any longer."

The Princess was so thirsty that she got down, bent over the stream, and drank, for she wasn't allowed the golden goblet. As she drank she murmured: "Oh! Heaven, what am I to do?" and the three drops of blood replied:

"If your mother only knew,
  Her heart would surely break in two."

But the Princess was meek, and said nothing about her maid's rude behavior, and quietly mounted her horse again. They rode on their way for several miles, but the day was hot, and the sun's rays smote fiercely on them, so that the Princess was soon overcome by thirst again. And as they passed a brook she called once more to her waiting-maid: "Pray get down and give me a drink from my golden cup," for she had long forgotten her maid's rude words.

But the waiting-maid replied, more haughtily than before:

"I Don't Mean to be Your Servant Any Longer."

"If you want a drink, you can dismount and get it; I don't mean to be your servant."

Then the Princess was compelled by her thirst to get down, and bending over the flowing water she cried and said: "Oh, heaven, what am I to do?" and the three drops of blood replied:

"If your mother only knew,
  Her heart would surely break in two."

And as she drank thus, and leant right over the water, the rag containing the three drops of blood fell from her bosom and floated down the stream, and she in her anxiety never even noticed her loss.

But the waiting-maid had observed it with delight, as she knew it gave her power over the bride, for in losing the drops of blood the Princess had become weak and powerless.

When she wished to get on her horse Falada again, the waiting-maid called out: "I mean to ride Falada: you must mount my beast;" and this too she had to submit to.

Then the waiting-maid harshly commanded the Princess to take off her royal robes, and to put on her own common ones, and finally she made her swear by heaven not to say a word about the matter when they reached the palace; and if she hadn't taken this oath she would have been killed on the spot. But Falada observed everything, and laid it all to heart.

The waiting-maid now mounted Falada, and the real bride the worse horse, and so they continued their journey till at length

"If Your Mother Only Knew..."

they arrived at the palace yard. There was great rejoicing over the arrival, and the Prince sprang forward to meet them, and taking the waiting-maid for his bride, he lifted her down from her horse and led her upstairs to the royal chamber.

In the meantime the real Princess was left standing below in the courtyard. The old King, who was looking out of his window, beheld her in this plight, and it struck him how sweet and gentle, even beautiful, she looked. He went at once to the royal chamber, and asked the bride who it was she had brought with her and had left thus standing in the court below.

"Oh!" replied the bride, "I brought her with me to keep me company on the journey; give the girl something to do, that she mayn't be idle."

But the old King had no work for her, and couldn't think of anything; so he said, "I've a small boy who looks after the geese, she'd better help him." The youth's name was Curdken, and the real bride was made to assist him in herding geese.

Soon after this the false bride said to the Prince: "Dearest husband, I pray you grant me a favor." He answered: "That I will."

"Let the slaughterer cut off the head of the horse I rode here upon, because it behaved very badly on the journey." But the truth was, she was afraid lest the horse should speak and tell how she had treated the Princess. She carried her point, and the faithful Falada was doomed to die.

When the news came to the ears of the real Princess she went

The Real Princess Was Standing Below.

to the slaughterer, and secretly promised him a piece of gold if he would do something for her.

There was in the town a large dark gate, through which she had to pass night and morning with the geese; would he kindly hang up Falada's head there, that she might see it once again? The slaughterer said he would do as she desired, chopped off the head, and nailed it firmly over the gateway.

Early next morning, as she and Curdken were driving their flock through the gate, she said as she passed under:

"Oh! Falada, 'tis you hang there;"
and the head replied:

" 'Tis you; pass under, Princess fair:
     If your mother only knew,
     Her heart would surely break in two."

Then she left the tower and drove the geese into a field. And when they had reached the common where the geese fed, she sat down and unloosed her hair, which was of pure gold. Curdken loved to see it glitter in the sun, and wanted much to pull some hair out. Then she spoke:

"Wind, wind, gently sway,
     Blow Curdken's hat away;
     Let him chase o'er field and wold
     Till my locks of ruddy gold,
     Now astray and hanging down,
     Be combed and braided in a crown."

She and Curdken Were Driving Their Flock.

Then a gust of wind blew Curdken's hat away, and he had to chase it over hill and dale. When he returned from the pursuit she had finished her combing and curling, and his chance of getting any hair was gone. Curdken was very angry, and wouldn't speak to her. So they herded the geese till evening and then went home.

The next morning, as they passed under the gate, the girl said:

"Oh! Falada, 'tis you hang there;"

and the head replied:

"'Tis you; pass under, Princess fair:

If your mother only knew,

Her heart would surely break in two."

Then she went on her way till she came to the common, where she sat down and began to comb out her hair; then Curdken ran up to her and wanted to grasp some of the hair from her head, but she called out hastily:

"Wind, wind, gently sway,

Blow Curdken's hat away;

Let him chase o'er field and wold

Till my locks of ruddy gold,

Now astray and hanging down,

Be combed and braided in a crown."

Then a puff of wind came and blew Curdken's hat far away, so that he had to run after it; and when he returned she had long finished putting up her golden locks, and he couldn't get any hair; so they watched the geese till it was dark.

A Gust of Wind Blew Curdken's Hat Away.

But that evening when they returned to the palace Curdken went to the old King, and said: "I refuse to herd geese any longer with that girl."

"For what reason?" asked the old King.

"Because she does nothing but annoy me all day long," replied Curdken; and he proceeded to relate all her doings, and he said: "Every morning as we drive the flock through the dark gate she says to a horse's head that hangs on the wall:

'Oh! Falada, 'tis you hang there;'
and the head replies:

"'Tis you; pass under, Princess fair:
If your mother only knew,
Her heart would surely break in two.'"

And Curdken went on to tell what passed on the common where the geese fed, and how he always had to chase his hat.

The old King bade him go and drive forth his flock as usual the next day; when morning came he himself took up a position behind the dark gate, and heard how the goose-girl greeted Falada. Then he followed her through the field, and hid himself behind a bush on the common. He soon saw with his own eyes how the goose-boy and the goose-girl looked after the geese, and how after a time the maiden sat down and loosed her hair, that glittered like gold, and repeated:

"Wind, wind, gently sway,
Blow Curdken's hat away;

Curdken Went to the Old King.

Let him chase o'er field and wold
Till my locks of ruddy gold,
Now astray and hanging down,
Be combed and braided in a crown."

Then a gust of wind came and blew Curdken's hat away, so that he had to fly over hill and dale after it, and the girl in the meantime quietly combed and braided her hair. All this the old King observed, and returned to the palace without any one having noticed him. In the evening when the goose-girl returned he called her aside, and asked her why she behaved as she did.

"I mayn't tell you why; how dare I confide my woes to anyone? For I swore not to by heaven, otherwise I should have lost my life," the real Princess replied.

The old King begged her to tell him all, and left her no peace, but he could get nothing out of her. At last he said: "Well, if you won't tell me, confide your trouble to the iron stove there;" and he went away.

Then she crept to the stove, and began to sob and cry and to pour out her poor little heart, and said: "Here I sit, deserted by all the world, I who am a King's daughter. A false waiting-maid has forced me to take off my own clothes, and has taken my place with my bridegroom, while I have to fulfill the lowly office of goose-girl.

"If my mother only knew,
Her heart would surely break in two."

But the old King stood outside at the stove chimney, and lis-

All This the Old King Observed.

tened to her words. Then he entered the room again, and bidding her leave the stove, he ordered royal apparel to be put on her, in which she looked amazingly lovely. Then he summoned his son, and revealed to him that he had got the false bride, who was nothing but a waiting-maid, while the real one, in the guise of the ex-goose-girl, was standing at his side.

The young Prince rejoiced from his heart when he saw her beauty and learnt how good she was, and a great banquet was prepared, to which everyone was bidden. The bridegroom sat at the head of the table, the Princess on one side of him and the waiting-maid on the other; but she was so dazzled that she did not recognize the Princess in her glittering garments.

Now when they had eaten and drunk, and were merry, the old King asked the waiting-maid to solve a knotty point for him. "What," said he, "should be done to a certain person who has deceived everyone?" And he proceeded to relate the whole story, ending up with, "Now what sentence should be passed?"

Then the false bride answered: "She deserves to be put into a barrel, which should be dragged by two white horses up and down the streets till she is dead."

"You are the person," said the King, "and you have passed sentence on yourself; and even so it shall be done to you."

And when the sentence had been carried out, the young Prince was married to his real bride, and both reigned over the kingdom in peace and happiness.

The Young Prince Rejoiced from His Heart.

She Cut Off a Shining Tress.

DORANI

O nce upon a time there lived a seller of scents and essences,
who had a very beautiful daughter named Dorani. This
maiden had a friend who was a fairy, and the two were high
in favor with Indra, the ruler of fairyland, because they were able
to sing so sweetly and dance so deftly that no one in the kingdom
could equal them for grace and beauty.

Dorani had the most lovely hair in the world, for it was like
spun gold, and the smell of it was like the smell of fresh roses. But
her locks were so long and thick that the weight of it was often
unbearable, and one day she cut off a shining tress, and wrapping
it in a large leaf, threw it in the river which ran just below her
window.

Now it happened that the King's son was out hunting, and
had gone down to the river to drink, when there floated towards
him a folded leaf, from which came a perfume of roses. The
Prince, with idle curiosity, took a step into the water and caught
the leaf as it was sailing by. He opened it, and within he found a

lock of hair like spun gold, from which came a faint, exquisite odor.

When the Prince reached home that day he looked so sad and was so quiet that his father wondered if any ill had befallen him, and asked what was the matter.

Then the youth took from his breast the tress of hair which he had found in the river, and holding it up to the light, replied: "See, my father, was ever hair like this? Unless I may win and marry the maiden that owns that lock I must die!"

So the King immediately sent heralds throughout all his dominions to search for the damsel with hair like spun gold, and at last he learned that she was the daughter of the scent-seller. The object of the herald's mission was quickly told abroad, and Dorani heard it with the rest; and, one day, she said to her father:

"If the hair is mine, and the King requires me to marry his son, I must do so; but, remember, you must tell him that if, after the wedding, I stay all day at the palace, every night will be spent in my old home."

The old man listened to her with amazement, but answered nothing, as he knew she was wiser than he. Of course the hair was Dorani's, and the heralds soon returned and informed the King, their master, who summoned the scent-seller, and told him that he wished for his daughter to be given in marriage to the Prince.

The father bowed his head three times, and replied: "Your highness is our lord, and all that you bid us we will do. The maiden

"Unless I Win That Maiden, I Die!"

asks this only — that if, after the wedding, she stays all day at the palace, she may go back each night to her father's house."

The King thought this a very strange request; but said to himself it was, after all, his son's affair, and the girl would surely soon get tired of going to and fro. So he made no difficulty, and everything was speedily arranged and the wedding was celebrated with great rejoicing.

At first, the condition attached to his wedding with the lovely Dorani troubled the Prince very little, for he thought that he would at least see his bride all day. But, to his dismay, he found that she would do nothing but sit the whole time upon a stool with her head bowed forward upon her knees, and he could never persuade her to say a single word.

Each evening she was carried in a palanquin to her father's house, and each morning she was brought back soon after daybreak; and yet never a sound passed her lips, nor did she show by any sign that she saw, or heard, or heeded her husband.

One evening the Prince, very unhappy and troubled, was wandering in an old and beautiful garden near the palace. The gardener was a very aged man, who had served the Prince's great-grandfather, and when he saw the Prince he came and bowed to him, and said:

"Child! Child! Why do you look so sad — what is the matter?"

The Prince replied: "I am sad, old friend, because I have married a wife as lovely as the stars, but she will not speak to me,

The Wedding was Celebrated with Great Rejoicing.

and I know not what to do. Night after night she leaves me for her father's house, and day after day she sits in mine as though turned to stone, and utters no word, whatever I may do or say."

The old man stood thinking for a moment, and then he hobbled off to his own cottage. A little later he came back to the Prince with five or six small packets, which he placed in his hands and said:

"Tomorrow, when your bride leaves the palace, sprinkle the powder from one of these packets upon your body, and while seeing clearly, you yourself will become invisible. More I cannot do for you, but may all go well!"

And the Prince thanked him, and put the packets carefully away.

The next night, when Dorani left for her father's house in her palanquin, the Prince took out a packet of the magic powder and sprinkled it over himself, and then hurried after her. He soon found that, as the old man had promised, he was invisible to everyone, although he felt as usual, and could see all that passed. He speedily overtook the palanquin and walked beside it to the scent-seller's dwelling. There it was set down, and, when his bride, closely veiled, left it and entered the house, he, too, entered unperceived.

At the first door Dorani removed one veil; then she entered another doorway at the end of a passage where she removed another veil; next she mounted the stairs, and at the door of the

"Day After Day She Sits as Though Turned to Stone."

women's quarters removed a third veil. After this she proceeded to her own room where were set two large basins, one of attar of roses and one of water; in these she washed herself, and afterwards called for food. A servant brought her a bowl of curds, which she ate hastily, and then arrayed herself in a robe of silver, and wound about her strings of pearls, while a wreath of roses crowned her hair.

When fully dressed, she seated herself upon a four-legged stool over which was a canopy with silken curtains; these she drew around her, and then called out:

"Fly, stool, to the palace of King Indra."

Instantly the stool rose in the air, and the invisible Prince, who had watched all these proceedings with great wonder, seized it by one leg as it flew away, and found himself being borne through the air at a rapid rate.

In a short while they arrived at the house of the fairy who, as mentioned before, was the favorite friend of Dorani. The fairy stood waiting on the threshold, as beautifully dressed as Dorani herself was, and when the stool stopped at her door she cried in astonishment:

"Why, the stool is flying all crooked to-day! What is the reason of that, I wonder? I suspect that you have been talking to your husband, and so it will not fly straight."

But Dorani declared that she had not spoken one word to him, and she couldn't think why the stool flew as if weighed down at one side. The fairy still looked doubtful, but made no answer,

"Fly, Stool, to the Palace of King Indra."

and took her seat beside Dorani, the Prince again holding tightly to one leg. Then the stool flew on through the air until it came to the palace of Indra.

All through the night the women sang and danced before the King Indra, whilst a magic lute played of itself the most bewitching music; till the Prince, who sat watching it all, was quite entranced. Just before dawn the King gave the signal to cease; and again the two women seated themselves on the stool, and, with the Prince clinging to the leg, it flew back to earth, and bore Dorani and her husband safely to the scent-seller's shop.

Here the Prince hurried away by himself past Dorani's palanquin with its sleepy bearers, straight on to the palace; and as he passed the threshold of his own rooms he became visible again. Then he awaited Dorani's arrival.

As soon as she arrived, she took a seat and remained as silent as usual, with her head bowed on her knees. For a while not a sound was heard, but presently the Prince said:

"I dreamed a curious dream last night, and as it was all about you I am going to tell it you, although you heed nothing."

The girl, indeed, took no notice of his words, but in spite of that he proceeded to relate every single thing that had happened the evening before, leaving out no detail of all that he had seen or heard.

And when he praised her singing — and his voice shook a little — Dorani just looked at him; but she said naught, though,

The Women Sang and Danced.

in her own mind, she was filled with wonder. "What a dream!" she thought. "Could it have been a dream? How could he have learnt in a dream all I did and said?" Still she kept silent; she only looked that once at the Prince, and then remained all day as before, with her head bowed upon her knees.

When night came the Prince again made himself invisible and followed her. The same things happened again as had happened before, but Dorani sang better than ever. In the morning the Prince a second time told Dorani all that she had done, pretending that he had dreamt of it. Directly after he finished, Dorani gazed at him, and said:

"Is it true that you dreamt this, or were you really there?"

"I was there," answered the Prince.

"But why do you follow me?" asked Dorani.

"Because," replied the Prince, "I love you, and to be with you is happiness."

This time Dorani's eyelids quivered, but she said no more, and was silent the rest of the day. However, in the evening, just as she was stepping into her palanquin, she said to the Prince: "If you love me, prove it by not following me tonight."

And so the Prince did as she wished, and stayed at home.

That evening the magic stool flew so unsteadily that they could hardly keep their seats, and at last the fairy exclaimed:

"There is only one reason that it should jerk like this! You have been talking to your husband!"

Her Head Bowed Upon Her Knees

And Dorani replied: "Yes, I have spoken; oh, yes, I have spoken!" But no more would she say.

That night Dorani sang so marvelously that at the end the King Indra rose up and vowed that she might ask what she would and he would give it to her. At first she was silent; but, when he pressed her, she answered: "Give me the magic lute."

The King, when he heard this, was displeased with himself for having made so rash a promise, because this lute he valued above all his possessions. But as he had promised, so he must perform, and with an ill grace he handed it to her.

"You must never come here again," said he, "for, once having asked so much, how will you in future be content with smaller gifts?"

Dorani bowed her head silently as she took the lute, and passed with the fairy out of the great gate, where the stool awaited them. More unsteadily than before, it flew back to earth.

When Dorani got to the palace that morning she asked the Prince whether he had dreamt again. He laughed with happiness, for this time she had spoken to him of her own free will; and he replied:

"No; but I begin to dream now — not of what *has* happened in the past, but of what *may* happen in the future."

That day Dorani sat very quietly, but she answered the Prince when he spoke to her; when evening fell, and with it the time for her departure, she still sat on. Then the Prince came close to her and said softly:

"Give Me the Magic Lute."

"Are you not going to your house, Dorani?"

At that she rose and threw herself weeping into his arms, whispering gently:

"Never again, my lord, never again would I leave thee!"

So the Prince won his beautiful bride; and though neither of them dealt any further with fairies and their magic, they learnt more daily of the magic of love, which one may still learn, although fairy magic has fled away.

"Never Again Would I Leave Thee!"

"Get Me Some Money Out of the Chest."

LITTLE · WILDROSE

O nce upon a time, there lived a man a hundred years old, if not twenty years more. And his wife was very old, too.

Old though they were, they had never made up their minds to do without children, and often talked of if only some had come to their house.

One day the old man said to his wife: "Listen to me, old woman! Get me some money out of the chest, for I am going all through the world to see if I can find us a child."

He took a bag and filled it with food and money, and throwing it over his shoulder, bade his wife farewell.

One morning his wanderings led him to a forest so thick with trees that no light could pass. Summoning up all his courage he plunged boldly in.

At last he reached a cave where the darkness seemed a hundred times darker than the wood itself. He felt as if something was driving him to enter, and with heart beating hard, he stepped in. Then he made a great effort and suddenly he saw a glimmer of light: he directed his steps towards it till he saw an old hermit, with a long white beard.

The old man fell on his knees. "Good morning, holy father!"

"My son," whispered the hermit, in a voice that echoed through the cavern, "what brings you to this dark and dismal place?"

"I have no child, and all our lives my wife and I have longed for one," replied the old man.

The hermit picked up an apple, saying: "Eat half of this apple, give the rest to your wife, and cease your wandering."

The old man made his way through the forest and at length arrived in flowery fields, when suddenly he was seized with a desperate thirst, a burning in his throat, and his tongue grew more parched every moment.

His eyes fell on the apple, which he had been holding in his hand, and he forgot what the hermit had told him, and instead of eating his own half, he ate up the old woman's also, and went to sleep.

When he woke up he saw, lying on a bank amidst long trails of pink roses, a little girl about two years old, as pink and white as the roses above her.

He took her gently in his arms, and set off for home as fast as his legs would carry him.

Close to the cottage he put her in a pail near the door, and ran crying: "Quickly, wife, I have brought you a daughter, with

"Eat Half of This Apple . . ."

hair of gold and eyes like stars!"

The old woman flew downstairs in her eagerness to see the treasure; but when her husband led her to the pail it was perfectly empty!

The old man was nearly beside himself with horror, while his wife sobbed with disappointment. There was not a spot they did not search, but the little girl was not there, and there was no sign of her.

And what had become of the baby? Well, finding herself alone in a strange place she began to cry, and an eagle hovering near heard her. When he beheld the pink and white creature he thought of his hungry little ones, and he caught her up in his claws and flew with her over the tops of the trees.

In a few minutes he reached his nest, and laying little Wildrose (for so the old man had called her) among his downy young eaglets, he flew away.

The eaglets naturally were rather surprised at this strange animal, so suddenly popped down in their midst, but instead of beginning to eat her, as their father expected, they nestled up close to her and spread out their tiny wings to shield her from the sun.

In the morning the eagle returned.

The sunbeam struggled through the thick branches and caught Wildrose's golden hair as she lay curled up in the corner, and the eagle said, "I brought her here for your dinner, and you have not touched her; what is the meaning of this?"

Wildrose opened her eyes, and seemed seven times lovelier

A Girl as Pink and White as the Roses

than before. From that day Wildrose lived like a little princess. The eagle collected the softest moss to make her a bed, and then he picked all the brightest and prettiest flowers in the fields or on the mountains to decorate it. There was not a fairy in the forest who would not have been pleased to sleep there, rocked to and fro by the breeze on the treetops.

When the little eaglets were able to fly from their nest, he taught them to look for the fruits and berries which she loved.

So time passed by, and Wildrose grew taller and more beautiful, living happily in her nest and never wanting to go out of it, only standing at the edge and looking upon the beautiful world.

For company she had all the birds in the forest, who talked to her, and for playthings the flowers that they brought her and the butterflies that danced with her. And so the days slipped away, and she was fourteen years old.

One morning the Emperor's son went out to hunt, and had not ridden far, before a deer ran before him. The Prince instantly gave chase, till at length he found himself in the depths of the forest, where no man before had trod.

The trees were so thick and the wood so dark, that he paused for a moment and listened, straining his ears to break the silence which almost frightened him. But nothing came. He stood still, and wondered if he should go on, when, on looking up, a stream of light seemed to flow from the top of a tall tree. In its rays he could see a nest with young eaglets.

He Caught Her Up in His Claws.

The Prince fitted an arrow into his bow and took aim, but before he could let fly, another ray of light dazzled him; so brilliant, that his bow dropped, and he covered his face with his hands. When at last he ventured to peep, Wildrose, with her golden hair flowing round her, was looking at him. This was the first time she had seen a man.

"Tell me how I can reach you!" cried he; but Wildrose smiled and shook her head, and sat down quietly.

The Prince saw that it was no use, and turned and made his way out of the forest. But he might as well have stayed there, for any good he was, so full was his heart with longing for Wildrose. Twice he returned to the forest in the hopes of finding her, but fortune failed him, and he went home as sad as ever.

At length the Emperor sent for his son and asked him what was the matter. Then the Prince confessed that the image of Wildrose filled his soul, and that he would never be happy without her.

At first the Emperor felt rather distressed. He doubted whether a girl from a tree top would make a good Empress; but he loved his son so much that he promised to do all he could to find her. The next morning heralds were sent throughout the land to inquire if anyone knew where a maiden could be found who lived in a forest on the top of a tree, and to promise great riches and a place at court to any person who should find her.

But nobody knew. All the girls in the kingdom had their homes on the ground, and laughed at the notion of being brought

For Company, the Birds of the Forest

up in a tree. "A nice Empress she would make," they said, as the Emperor had done, tossing their heads with disdain.

The heralds were in despair, when an old woman stepped out of the crowd and spoke to them. She was very old, with a bald head, and when the heralds saw her they broke into rude laughter. "I can show you the maiden who lives in the tree top," she said, but they only laughed the more loudly.

"Get away, old witch!" they cried. "You will bring us bad luck." But the old woman stood firm, and declared that she alone knew where to find the maiden.

"Go with her," said the eldest of the heralds at last. "The Emperor's orders are clear, that whoever knew anything of the maiden was to come at once to court. Put her in the coach and take her with us." So the old woman was brought to court.

"You can bring the maiden from the wood?" said the Emperor.

"Yes, your Majesty, and I will," said she.

"Bring her at once," said the Emperor.

"Give me a kettle and a tripod," asked the old woman, and the Emperor ordered them instantly. She tucked them under her arm and went on her way, keeping at a little distance behind the royal huntsmen, who in turn followed the Prince.

Oh, what a noise that old woman made as she walked along! She chattered so fast and clattered her kettle so loudly that you would have thought that a whole band must be coming. But when

"Tell Me How I Can Reach You!"

they reached the forest, she bade them all wait outside, and entered the wood by herself.

She stopped underneath the tree where the maiden dwelt and kindled a fire. She placed the tripod over it, and the kettle on top. But something was the matter with the kettle. As fast as the old woman put it where it was to stand, that kettle was sure to roll off, falling to the ground with a crash.

It really seemed bewitched, and no one knows what might have happened if Wildrose, who had been peeping out of her nest, had not lost patience at the old woman's stupidity, and cried out: "The tripod won't stand on that hill, you must move it!"

"But where am I to move it to, my child?" asked the old woman, looking up to the nest, and at the same moment trying to steady the kettle with one hand and the tripod with the other.

"Didn't I tell you that it was no good doing that?" said Wildrose, more impatiently than before. "Make a fire near a tree and hang the kettle from one of the branches."

The old woman took the kettle and hung it on a little twig, which broke at once, and the kettle fell to the ground.

"If you would only show me how to do it, perhaps I would understand," said she.

Quick as thought, Wildrose slid down the tree trunk, and stood beside the stupid old woman, to teach her how things ought to be done.

But in an instant the old woman had caught her up and

"You Must Move It!"

swung her over her shoulders, and was running as fast as she could to the edge of the forest, where she had left the Prince.

When he saw them coming he rushed eagerly to meet them. He took the maiden in his arms and kissed her tenderly. Then a golden dress was put on her, and pearls were twined in her hair, and she took her seat in the Emperor's carriage, which was drawn by six of the whitest horses in the world, and they carried her, without stopping to draw breath, to the gates of the palace.

And in three days the wedding was celebrated, and the wedding feast was held, and everyone who saw the bride declared that if anybody wanted a perfect wife, they must go to seek her on top of a tree.

A Golden Dress Was Put on Her.